The

McNifficents

written by
AMY MAKECHNIE

Simon & Schuster Books for Young Readers
New York   London   Toronto   Sydney   New Delhi

SIMON & SCHUSTER BOOKS FOR YOUNG READERS

An imprint of Simon & Schuster Children's Publishing Division

1230 Avenue of the Americas, New York, New York 10020

SIMON & SCHUSTER BOOKS FOR YOUNG READERS

and related marks are trademarks of Simon & Schuster, Inc.

For information about special discounts for bulk purchases, please contact Simon & Schuster Special Sales at 1-866-506-1949 or business@simonandschuster.com.

The Simon & Schuster Speakers Bureau can bring authors to your live event.

For more information or to book an event, contact the Simon & Schuster Speakers Bureau at 1-866-248-3049 or visit our website at www.simonspeakers.com.

Interior design by Sarah Creech and Evelyn Wang

The text for this book was set in Adobe Caslon Pro.

The illustrations for this book were rendered digitally.

Manufactured in the United States of America

0523 FFG

First Edition

2 4 6 8 10 9 7 5 3 1

Library of Congress Cataloging-in-Publication Data

Names: Makechnie, Amy, author.

Title: The McNifficents / Amy Makechnie.

Description: First edition. | New York : Simon & Schuster Books for Young Readers, 2023.

Identifiers: LCCN 2022041867 (print) | LCCN 2022041868 (ebook) |

ISBN 9781665918985 (hardcover) | ISBN 9781665919005 (ebook)

Subjects: CYAC: Nannies—Fiction. | Miniature schnauzers—Fiction. | Dogs—Fiction. | Behavior—Fiction.

Classification: LCC PZ7.1.M34685 Mc 2023 (print) | LCC PZ7.1.M34685 (ebook) | DDC [Fic]—dc23

LC record available at https://lccn.loc.gov/2022041867

LC ebook record available at https://lccn.loc.gov/2022041868

For my own McNifficents:
Cope, Nelson, Brynne, and Paige—
and, of course, Lord Tennyson

CHAPTER ONE

The McNiffs Go to the Beach

IN A LARGE PINK FARMHOUSE AT 238 MARIGOLD Lane lives a most unusual nanny: Lord Tennyson, a short, middle-aged gentleman with white whiskers and a royal pedigree. If he could speak, it would be with dignity and a touch of an English accent. If he wore clothing, he imagines he'd wear a suit of gray silk and a striped bow tie. But he does neither because Lord Tennyson is a dog, a miniature schnauzer to be exact, who wears only a blue-and-green collar that has teeth marks in it from when Sweetums was going through a particularly bad biting phase.

Despite his distinguished appearance and pedigree, he was not spending his morning caring for a dignitary's son or the daughter of the president. Rather, his duty was herding the unruly McNiff children from the old pink farmhouse into the old red farm truck for the first swim of summer vacation. There were six of them: two boys and four girls. As you can imagine, getting all of them to and from the lake was not an easy task. There were swimsuits, sunscreen, towels, toys, and countless cheese sticks to pack. (Lord Tennyson loved cheese sticks, so he packed a few extra for himself.) There was whining and shushing and clambering and squishing into one another as the children jockeyed for their favorite grubby, crumb-filled seats. There was yanking on seat belts or trying to disregard them altogether until Lord Tennyson's stern, reprimanding eyebrow demanded buckling.

By the time they finally set off, Lord Tennyson was already panting from the incredible effort and early-morning heat. (After all, he always wore a lovely coat of fur.) He settled onto nine-year-old Ezra's lap, relishing in his favorite part of any ride: sticking his head out the window and allowing his tongue to flap in the wind. Long strings of drool trailed behind, which was a completely undignified look, but without a linen handkerchief, unavoidable.

This luxury did not last long. Lord Tennyson, always in high demand, was immediately snatched off Ezra's lap by eleven-year-old Mary.

"Oh, sweet baby," Mary cooed, holding him like *he* was the infant and scratching his stomach.

Lord Tennyson did not appreciate being yanked and grabbed. Also, he was not a "sweet baby." Yet he understood that humans had a great need to baby talk to furry, adorable creatures like himself. He also tolerated most anything from his charges for belly scratches.

"I had Tenny first," Ezra said, pulling him back off Mary's lap. Mary frowned, her brown eyes narrowing behind her cat-eyed frames.

Mrs. McNiff, whom Lord Tennyson called Honey (because that was what Mr. McNiff called her), glanced in the rearview mirror expectantly. This was Lord Tennyson's cue to wriggle loose, shake out his fur, and step firmly between the two children. But before he could distract

Mary, she whispered, "Don't be surprised, Ezzie, if you find yourself in a hole tomorrow morning!" This, you see, was exactly the type of bad-mannered behavior that had earned her the title of "Naughty Mary."

Honey, who did not quite have the keen sense of hearing that Lord Tennyson had, smiled approvingly at him as they rumbled down the dusty country road. Despite the squabbling, Lord Tennyson's confidence was sure. No, his task was not an easy one, as worthwhile work never is, but he did not doubt his child-rearing abilities, for he knew he was a rather spectacular dog. And clearly, Honey knew it too, which made his heart swell.

When they arrived, the children ran across the beach sand, but Lord Tennyson stopped short. He was not allowed on the town beach. There was a large sign that said so. Though the rules were unfair, Lord Tennyson followed them because he knew children modeled their behavior after their caretakers. Oh yes, he would have liked to race the children, feel the warm sand under his paws, the wind in his fur. But then again, he did not swim. In fact, he hated getting wet. The only time he enjoyed water was when he was drinking it. So perhaps it was all for the best.

Lord Tennyson obeyed the sign and trotted over to his favorite lilac bush with the good vantage point, ready to lie down beneath the fragrant branches. He wanted to nap, but he was on duty, and when at the lake, he was like a hawk tracking a mouse, especially when it came to Sweetums, who had a propensity for sand-throwing and near-drowning episodes.

At eighteen months, Sweetums was the baby of the family, and like most babies, she was very spoiled. With a name like "Sweetums" and a small fountain of angelic blond curls sprouting from the top of her head, she was often mistaken for having an angelic personality. If you knew Sweetums, "angelic" would not be the word you would use to describe her. And in truth, most times it was only her extreme cuteness that kept her alive.

Lord Tennyson lay with his head on his paws, watching her crawl across the sand, away from Honey and her brothers and sisters. He made a mental note: this was the summer he had to teach that baby to walk. After all, she was practically a toddler, and still being carried around by himself and her siblings! He raised his head when Sweetums made a sharp left turn and charged toward the water.

She took big licks of water until she choked and spit half the lake out her nose. Lord Tennyson's ears twitched. Goodness, would she never learn? Just last week he had fished her out of a cleaning bucket after she had decided to stick her head in to blow bubbles. Perhaps he should hold off on the walking lessons, as she was liable to get into even more trouble if mobile.

Sweetums moved away from the water, and Lord Tennyson relaxed. Again his peace was short-lived, as who should he see coming down the beach path but Mrs. Snoot! As usual, Mrs. Snoot did not look like she was having a good day. In one hand she held a giant umbrella, a chair, and a small cooler stocked with sugary beverages. With her other hand she dragged her two small Snoot children, parking herself as far away from the McNiffs as possible. Not wanting to be seen by the Snoots, he backed farther beneath the lilac bush.

Over the next hour, the quiet beach filled with parents, babysitters, chattering children, and the McNiffs' friends, including Cal Hubbard. Lord Tennyson knew rest time was officially over. Thirteen-year-old Annie, the oldest and most responsible McNiff child, was Sweetums's official "buddy," but with Cal on the beach, Annie's brain was officially mush.

As if on cue, Sweetums, seemingly bored with licking the water, began peeling off her swimsuit, preferring to wander the world completely unclothed. (Lord Tennyson acknowledged that he too was unclothed, but only because he'd never been offered the refined tuxedo he dreamed of.) Sweetums tugged and pulled until the swimsuit was bundled into a wet, sandy ball, then flung it behind her, where it landed on Mrs. Snoot's large, purple-painted toenail.

Mrs. Snoot squeaked out a horrible noise and flung it off like a disease.

Sweetums stood, wobbled, and pounded her chest like a baby gorilla. She then went to work on removing her diaper. Lord Tennyson cringed at the sight. Sweetums's backside was already so swollen with lake water, it looked like a giant water balloon was hanging from her bottom. Despite his many nudges that morning, Honey had forgotten the swim diapers. With so many children to look after, she often forgot essential items like this.

Frustrated with the diaper she was unable to get off,

Sweetums instead flung herself into the water. Lord Tennyson glanced at Honey, who was reapplying sunscreen to a squirming Mary. Annie, flanked by two school friends, was laughing over something Cal had just said. Ezra was playing shark with his new goggles, and Pearl and Tate were blissfully unaware of anything that wasn't Pearl's favorite Barbie doll, a boy she had named Nicholas.

There wasn't a moment to lose. The rules would have to be broken.

Lord Tennyson dashed across the sand, past Mrs. Snoot's purple toenails, and hauled the monstrous diaper and squirming child out of the lake.

Sweetums choked and sprayed more water out of her nose before yelling, "Again, Ten Ten!" He gagged, sure he would never *ever* get the taste of soggy diaper off his tongue.

When they reached the shore again, Lord Tennyson shook, spraying cold lake water all over Sweetums . . . and unfortunately, Mrs. Snoot.

"Oh, oh, oh!" Mrs. Snoot shrieked. "I'm wet!"

Her children looked at him, delighted.

"It's *that* animal!" Mrs. Snoot yelled, rising. "It's on

the beach *again*! GET!" Since Honey was finally hurrying across the sand to help and he wanted to avoid the wrath of the purple toenails, he bolted back to his lilac bush.

Honey picked up Sweetums, looking distressed at the state of her diaper, now three times its normal size and torn in the back where Lord Tennyson had grabbed it with his teeth.

As Honey apologized to Mrs. Snoot, it became clear that unfortunately, Lord Tennyson's gallantry had exposed his hiding spot to a swarm of small children nearby, who began petting him and trying to feed him rocks. He tolerated the crowd of small humans because he was a gentleman, though truthfully, Lord Tennyson did not like most children who were not the McNiffs. Children had perpetually sticky fingers, spoke too loudly, and thought pulling his little stub of a tail was hysterical. And now they were distracting him from his important responsibilities!

At that very moment hands closed around his throat, squeezing. Lord Tennyson felt his eyes bulge as he was rolled over onto the grass and sat on. He knew this small beast all too well: the maniacal giggle, buzz cut, and large front teeth sticking out from a round freckled face. Curtis Cornell.

Curtis bounced on Lord Tennyson's stomach and shouted, "Giddyap!"

"Leave the doggy alone," his mother said absently, looking at her phone. Ugh, if there was one word Lord Tennyson could not abide, it was "doggy." He managed to wriggle out from underneath the pretend cowboy and played "Dodge Curtis Cornell" until Curtis was too hot to "giddyap" and the boy ran into the water.

Lord Tennyson panted wearily and quickly counted the curly-topped heads of all six McNiff children, hoping nothing had befallen them while he was being harassed. The three oldest were in the water; Sweetums was tasting the sand, spitting, and yelling "yummy"; and Pearl and Tate were burying Nicholas under the sand. This did not bode well, as they had a habit of losing their dolls when burying them.

He was so intent on memorizing the burial spot that he missed dodging Curtis Cornell's next sneak attack.

"Got you, dog. I got you!" Curtis shouted as he tackled Lord Tennyson to the ground.

Lord Tennyson watched helplessly from underneath Curtis Cornell as the doll was buried and Sweetums scooped up a handful of sand, clearly ready for a second round of trouble. She scooted on her gigantic ripped diaper until she came to Mrs. Snoot, who had just been buried under the sand by her children and now lay with a sleep mask over her eyes.

Lord Tennyson wiggled and squirmed, but Curtis now had him in a headlock. Sweetums crawled closer and closer to Mrs. Snoot, smiling angelically—but there was mischief in her eyes. There was only one thing Lord Tennyson could do: he bucked like a bull rider and bounced Curtis into the lilac bush.

"Ah-h-h-h-h-h!"

"Curtis Cornell!" his mother said, finally looking up. "Get out of that bush!"

"The doggy did it!" Curtis howled. *"Doggy" again!*

"Don't be ridiculous," his mother shouted.

"I'll get you, dog! I'll get you!" Curtis yelled.

But Lord Tennyson was already running to the edge of the sand. Sweetums was now a foot away from Mrs. Snoot. The Snoot children looked at her and smiled, inviting her to play, while Lord Tennyson yelped to discourage it.

Sweetums crawled farther forward.

Mrs. Snoot began to snore while Sweetums plopped a fistful of sand onto Mrs. Snoot's sand-covered stomach. Lord Tennyson held his breath. That wasn't so bad, he supposed. Perhaps Sweetums was actually entering a new phase, like playing nicely with others. Mrs. Snoot's entire body was already covered with sand except for her neck and head. How much harm could Sweetums cause?

But as if she had heard his thoughts, Sweetums crawled over to Mrs. Snoot's head.

Oh no.

Using her hands to balance on the ground, Sweetums very carefully stood. Lord Tennyson frantically looked for Honey, but she was watching the water as the other children played.

And to make matters worse, Mrs. Snoot, perhaps feeling the presence of a twenty-five-pound toddler hovering over her head, suddenly snorted herself awake.

"Who's that?" she asked drowsily, mask still covering her eyes.

Sweetums crouched and picked up two heaping handfuls of sand.

Once again, Lord Tennyson was forced to break the

rules. He leaped over towels, cold cuts, and a flock of birds on his way to stop Sweetums (which was a great sacrifice, as birds were his most favorite snack).

Mrs. Snoot wriggled until her hand was free and she could remove her sleep mask. She opened her eyes, squinting at the bright light.

Lord Tennyson willed himself to run faster, but he was getting on in years and the gap wasn't closing fast enough.

He watched helplessly as Sweetums opened her fingers and released a fistful of sand right into Mrs. Snoot's now-open eyeballs. A terrific shriek echoed across the entire beach. The noise delighted Sweetums, who, upon seeing another open hole, dropped the other fistful of sand right into Mrs. Snoot's mouth.

Lord Tennyson, who had finally arrived, grabbed Sweetums once more by the back of her torn, waterlogged diaper and dragged her over to Honey. He set her down and looked pointedly at Honey as Mrs. Snoot's sand-muffled screams continued. It was time to go. Thankfully, Honey agreed, gathering the buckets and toys while Lord Tennyson corralled the other children for a quick getaway.

Anticipating the next hurdle to their speedy exit and somewhat confident he had the right burial spot, he began digging for Pearl's doll as the kids emerged from the water. But all he found was a tiny pair of pants.

"Nicholas!" Pearl wailed. "I've lost my Nicholas!"

"Leave him," Ezra said.

"We can't leave Nicholeth!" Tate said, his big eyes blinking behind his water-splattered red rubber glasses.

"It will teach you both a lesson to stop burying him," Annie said. "It's ridiculous that—"

"Need help?" Cal asked.

"Oh, no thanks," Annie said, her voice suddenly as sweet as her mother's name.

"I've lost my boy!" Pearl cried. "My most favorite boy."

Annie blushed the color of a ripe raspberry as Cal walked off.

Pearl wailed on the beach while Lord Tennyson alternated between digging and nudging the other children to move quickly before Mrs. Snoot had removed all the sand from her nose and eyes.

"I don't want to go," Mary said, digging in her heels. "We just got here."

"It's Sweetums's fault," Ezra said. "And now we're getting kicked out—again!"

"You are all so embarrassing," Annie said.

"Tenny!" Pearl sobbed, digging alongside Lord Tennyson. "My Nicholas!"

"Your children are completely out of control!"

They were too late. Mrs. Snoot was suddenly upon them, pointing at Sweetums. Annie picked up her little sister and hugged her protectively.

While Honey dealt with Mrs. Snoot, Lord Tennyson put his superb sniffing skills to use. Nose to the ground, he finally caught the scent he was looking for. With a little digging, sure enough, a small plastic hand emerged. He dug further, using two paws to quickly unearth the doll.

"Nicholas!" Pearl cried as her treasured doll emerged in his polka-dot tuxedo—minus the pants.

"*Nicholas!*" Mary said dramatically, throwing a sand clod at Ezra.

Ezra threw a sand clod back.

The action ignited a chain reaction. It suddenly seemed that every child on the beach was throwing sand and whooping loudly. Lord Tennyson herded the McNiffs once more, appalled that his children were the cause of such beach-wide chaos but glad it also gave them a chance for a quick escape from the wrath of Mrs. Snoot, who was now dodging flying sand. As she did, she unleashed a full-blown rant about babies and dogs on the beach, ending with one final, insulting remark: *"Get those children a real nanny!"* As if he weren't standing right there! It deeply wounded Lord Tennyson, but what wounded him more was how Honey stopped in her tracks and tilted her head, as if she were actually considering Mrs. Snoot's words!

"I hate her!" Mary said darkly when they were safely in the truck. "Tenny, go bite her!"

Lord Tennyson frowned.

"She's Cruella de Vil!" Mary said. "If you want to keep your fur coat, stay far away."

Tate shrieked and clutched Tenny.

"Mary," Honey sighed. "No one's taking Tenny's fur. Mrs. Snoot had every reason to be angry."

While Lord Tennyson could see that, her comments about him and his beloved family cut deep. It occurred to him that humans got fired all the time—could *he* be? Where would he go? A senior dog home where the children visited him when they had nothing else to do? The thought of anyone other than himself raising the McNiffs gave him heart palpitations.

As Honey drove home down the long dirt road in the old truck, Lord Tennyson waited for her to continue with a stern talking-to, or to reassure him what a fine job he had done at the beach. Instead, Honey began to hum. Though Lord Tennyson was always happy to see Honey smiling, he was hoping for more firmness. But no, Honey had that dreamy, "I love asparagus" look in her eyes as she pulled into the driveway of their large pink farmhouse. A brilliant—though absent-minded—home chemist and master gardener, Honey was likely already envisioning the kale, carrots, and broccoli she would harvest for the children's lunch smoothie.

It was this quality that made her both good and patient with children, but it also made Lord Tennyson's service absolutely essential. Didn't she see that?

While Honey headed to the garden as soon as she'd parked, Lord Tennyson put his paw on the door lock and straightened up to his whole height (an impressive two feet). He faced the six children, his salt-and-pepper eyebrows solemnly raised.

"What's the matter, boy?" Ezra said. "We were just having fun."

"He's mad at Sweetums," Mary said. "For what she did." She said this in a pleased sort of way. For once, she wasn't the one in trouble.

"She threw thand in Mithuth Thnoot'th eyeth, right, Pearl?" Tate said.

"Oh, Sweetums," Annie said disapprovingly.

"What do you mean 'Oh, Sweetums'? She's *your* buddy," Mary said. "You weren't watching her."

"I *was!*"

"You were watching Cal," Ezra said. "Let's be serious."

"Shut up!" Annie said.

Pearl and Tate gasped. "Bad words!"

"Sut up," Sweetums said, banging her feet on the seat. "Sut up, sut up, sut up."

"Look what you taught her," Mary said gleefully.

Annie huffed, unlocked the door, and took Sweetums and her squishy, stuffing-escaping diaper into the house. Lord Tennyson watched the McNiffs empty out of the truck, his heart heavy at their unkind words and heavier still as he looked around the inside of the truck, strewn with toys, sand, smashed crackers, and wet towels. *A real nanny.* He nibbled on a sandy, half-eaten cheese stick on the floor, feeling a great urgency. This summer was essential, before it was too late and the McNiffs were forever lost to their messy ways and deplorable behavior. He couldn't let that happen. Not these children. Not *his* children.

Yes, Lord Tennyson was resolved. The easy golden years he'd begun to dream of were out of the question. There was no one else, despite what Mrs. Snoot had said, who could do what he must: tame the unruly, bad-mannered McNiff children before summer's end.

CHAPTER TWO

Annie's Discontent

THE NEXT MORNING LORD TENNYSON AWOKE EARLY.
It was a new day, and he was determined to start it well.
He had been doing his research on real nannies by watching *Mary Poppins*, after convincing Mr. McNiff to keep
the movie on last night, and was determined to emulate
the title character. Oh, how he adored her. He sought to
be her equal—fair, and not unkind, but certainly not nice.
Nannies weren't supposed to be nice. He meant to raise

respectful, obedient, and loving human beings who behaved well. Someday these children would be responsible for this world they lived in, and preparing for that all started right here in the McNiff home.

So today Lord Tennyson would start with the two basic yet very important morning tasks that he was still teaching the McNiff children:

1. Open the door to let him outside to do his business.

2. Feed him.

Alas, after all these years, the McNiffs still needed him to circle the earliest riser, then put his paw on the large tub of dog food that had a sign posted: DOG FOOD! NOT FOR SWEETUMS. Of course, he could figure out how to do these things himself, but this was about responsibility and the children caring for others as much as themselves.

He rose and stretched slowly, his joints stiff. He sniffed at something pungent in the air, then peeked over to where Tate, Pearl, and baby Sweetums lay sleeping in a very cramped bed. Sweetums had been leaping out of her crib for months, always preferring to find a sibling to squish in with. There was an extra single bed in Ezra's room, but after Ezra's tall tales of wolves living in closets had terrorized

Pearl, Tate slept protectively squished between his sisters, and often Lord Tennyson. The smell wasn't coming from their direction, though.

He sniffed again, putting his nose to the ground. There *was* a smell, and a great feeling of dread settled in Lord Tennyson's empty stomach. His dread was confirmed with an angry sigh and the sound of feet slapping the ground as they stomped down the hall.

"She did it again!" Annie hissed as he followed her into the bathroom. Her long brown hair was rolled into the pink sponge rollers she used to tame the wild McNiff hair. She attempted to peel off her long white nightgown, but it was soaked, sticking to her body with the source of the smell.

"She wet the bed *again*!"

Yes, Mary was the heaviest sleeper in the world and, unfortunately, was still wetting the bed she shared with her older sister. "This is why I can't ever have anyone spend the night!" Annie said.

Lord Tennyson tried to help by pulling at the hem of the nightgown with his teeth, but it only made Annie more frustrated until she finally hurled herself fully clothed into the shower and turned on the water. Lord Tennyson leaped back. He detested bathtime.

"Why, Tenny?" she moaned. "Why does she do this to me?"

Lord Tennyson shook his head in sympathy. Annie's nightgown *was* beautiful, and a gift from her grandmother, who had brought it back all the way from England and said it was in the style of Queen Elizabeth: white with an eyelet top, long sleeves, and a hem that went all the way down to Annie's ankles.

"Brrr!" she said, finally bursting out from behind the shower curtain. The water heater in the old farmhouse was on its last legs, and cold showers were the norm, making Lord Tennyson like them even less.

Annie went and changed, but before going downstairs with the hamper, she paused in the doorway of her shared room.

Together they surveyed the scene.

Annie's side of the room was tidy. The other side looked like a tornado had hit. Mary's clothes were hanging out of her dresser or on the floor. Books were scattered. An old apple core sat on the windowsill, brown and droopy.

"This is the last straw, Tenny," Annie whispered, more

to herself than him. "I'm thirteen years old and should not have to sleep with a bed-wetting baby. Mary's behavior *must* go before the Sibling Council."

Mary rolled over in bed, oblivious, while Lord Tennyson blinked. The Sibling Council was a brilliant idea . . . unless the agenda was solely for Annie to complain about Mary (which was usually the agenda). Last time, the meeting had abruptly ended with Mary emptying Lord Tennyson's water bowl over Annie's head. No one thought to refill it, so Lord Tennyson had been forced to drink out of Sweetums's cereal bowl, and *he* had gotten in trouble.

But before Lord Tennyson could question further whether this was truly a good idea, Annie stomped downstairs. Lord Tennyson took off, hot on her barefoot heels. The early-morning light was streaming through the kitchen window as the neighborhood rooster crowed.

Lord Tennyson circled Annie, beginning their first lesson, and she took the hint immediately. "Calm down, boy," Annie said, heading to open the back door. An excellent start, if he did say so himself.

He bounded out the back door and found his favorite

tree. There. Much better. The rooster crowed again, and Lord Tennyson, invigorated by his first success and the lovely summer morning—and perhaps also the sounds of birds—raced around the house twice before entering the back door through the torn screen, ready to eat.

Unfortunately, Annie had forgotten that part. He sat beneath the food and barked, but Annie was intent on making a point to her mother, who was now up and stuffing greens into a blender, magically turning them into a green-sludge breakfast smoothie. Honey was already wearing her gardening clothes, but sleep marks were still on her face and Annie's monologue was going unanswered.

Lord Tennyson paused his lesson to trot over to greet Honey good morning and let her know he was on duty, rubbing his cheek against her leg. Honey reached down and petted his head and ears in just the way he liked.

"*Mom,*" Annie said.

Honey held up her hand, gulped down the smoothie, and then smiled.

"There," she said. "Now the day may begin."

But before Annie could launch back into things, Honey handed her daughter her own glass of smoothie, slid on her gardening boots, and grabbed her wide-brimmed straw hat by the back door.

Annie swallowed a mouthful of the green drink and grimaced.

"Breakfast," Honey said, absent-mindedly indicating Lord Tennyson's empty dog bowl to Annie as she headed out. Lord Tennyson barked again, resuming his plan, and Annie paused . . . then poured her very green smoothie into his bowl.

He stared at it, glowering, then lapped it up. He shuddered from head to toe as he swallowed the green liquid that tasted like both a very sour lemon and grass clippings. He only wished Annie and Honey had stuck around to see his virtuous example.

Lord Tennyson caught up to Annie and Honey halfway across the backyard, his four legs becoming wet and bright green from the dewed grass. Mornings were his favorite part of a summer day, before he was too hot under his coat and while an abundance of tasty little birds were still playing and whistling. It was also when his nemesis neighbor, Fat Cat, was still lazily sleeping in and he didn't have to look at her smarmy grin.

So, as they trotted across the lawn, Lord Tennyson

relished the cool temperature, the yawning sunrise, and the possible adventures of the day ahead with the children. He had already forgotten Mary's bed-wetting problem.

Annie had not.

"Mom," Annie said. "I refuse to sleep with Mary another night!"

Honey took long strides across the grass while pulling on her gardening gloves. Lord Tennyson kept pace, privy to every conversation. Humans were always shutting the door on one another, but rarely on their dogs, likely because dogs were far better listeners than they were.

He thought this was certainly true with Honey as she responded with only, "Look at these sweet peas." Lord Tennyson sniffed at Honey to help her pay attention. But instead, Honey responded by plucking a pea pod off a tall stem and holding it out to him. He sniffed and chomped it down quickly, hoping to redirect her attention.

"Mom, I'm serious," Annie said. "I can't do it anymore. It's completely unfair!"

Oh, how Lord Tennyson wished she wouldn't go there. Fair didn't matter. This was just a problem in need of a solution. He stared at Annie, willing her to change strategy.

"I really can't do it anymore! She's ruining my life. I cannot wake up WET ONE MORE DAY! NOT ONE MORE!"

(The McNiff children took after their father a bit when it came to dramatics.)

Honey knelt in the dirt to pull a weed from her peas, but finally responded, "Annie, some children have a harder time waking up at night."

"Mom, she's eleven years old!"

Honey squinted into the sunlight. "Is that right?"

"Yes, and she's just too lazy to get up," Annie said.

Honey looked at Lord Tennyson for guidance.

Annie looked at him for support.

Lord Tennyson nodded solemnly, considering next steps.

"Lord Tennyson and I are in agreement!" Annie announced.

They were?

"She must be banished from my room," Annie said.

Lord Tennyson gave her a stern look. She knew it was their *shared* room and banishment was not the solution.

She paused, then tried again. "Isn't there something— *anything*—we could do to train her to get up?"

Better. He nodded, his gaze shifting to Honey.

"Well," Honey said, "just the other day I heard that Mr. Bellows is selling something called 'The Wet-Alarm.' Maybe next week . . ."

"Today," Annie said, jumping up. "It has to be today!"

"You're going to pick up our new baby chicks this morning. But I suppose beforehand your father could take you to check out this wet-alarm."

Annie clapped her hands.

"But, Annie—"

"What?"

"Be kind to Mary about it."

Annie nodded, dancing around, but stopped when the loud singing voice of Mr. McNiff floated across the backyard from the house. Today he was Don Quixote from *Man of La Mancha*, the musical he was directing this summer at the local community theater. Annie and Lord Tennyson took off running toward the house, racing to see their beloved Mr. McNiff, though Lord Tennyson couldn't shake the feeling that Annie hadn't really been listening to the kindness part of Honey's instructions.

CHAPTER THREE

Mary's Wet-Alarm

AN HOUR LATER, LORD TENNYSON WAS HERDING the children into the truck for their outing. It had been many years since the McNiffs had purchased new chicks! How incredibly exciting.

Mr. McNiff was accompanying them, smartly dressed in nicely pressed khakis and a pink pinstriped shirt. If he were a human, not a dignified dog, Lord Tennyson imagined that Mr. McNiff was exactly who he would be.

Oh yes, he loved Mr. McNiff's sharp clothes, his low baritone voice, and the way he relied on Lord Tennyson to run a shipshape home. He often imagined himself standing side by side with Mr. McNiff, dressed in matching suits and striped socks. Alas, the last article of clothing the McNiff children had gotten him besides his collar was something they called an ugly Christmas sweater. When they put it on him, they had howled with laughter. Mary Poppins would *never* have put up with that. It now lay safely buried under the deck.

Once the children were settled, Mr. McNiff started the old truck, but it sputtered and halted in the driveway.

"Punch it, Poopsie!" Mr. McNiff hollered, motivating the old truck to drive another day. Lord Tennyson sat sandwiched between Pearl and Tate as the truck began to rumble forward. When they drove past Mr. Goody's farm, Tate shouted, "What about our chickth?"

"First," Mr. McNiff said, pausing dramatically, "we have a very important purchase to make. Then we'll procure the chicks." The mention of "chicks" made Lord Tennyson's mouth water.

Mary stuck out her tongue at Annie, furious about the detour.

They parked at Bellows, the only grocery and all-purpose store in their small New Hampshire town. Bald Mr. Bellows owned it, and he always bellowed, true to his name. This morning, he was bellowing outside, directing a large delivery of bananas. Behind him was a sign.

"No dogs?" Pearl said, gasping and pointing to it as she jumped down from the truck. Lord Tennyson beamed, proud of how she was learning to read so well under his tutelage.

"It means Tenny isn't supposed to come in," Annie said.

"But that would only be true if he were a mere dog," Mr. McNiff said, opening the front door of the store with a flourish. "Tenny is no ordinary hound."

Lord Tennyson puffed out his fur-covered chest and marched behind Mr. McNiff. The two of them smiled at everyone and everyone smiled back.

While most dogs could not enter stores, Lord Tennyson's well-mannered reputation preceded him. And as their nanny, he was allowed—actually, encouraged—to accompany the McNiff children, as *their* reputation preceded them as well. He particularly liked the grocery store because the butcher often wrapped up a fresh bone for him.

Remembering his duty, he circled back to the children, putting his nose to Sweetums's stroller and helping Tate push it forward. Mary stomped behind them while Annie skipped gleefully. Lord Tennyson tried to ignore the foreboding deep in his stomach.

While Mr. McNiff was immediately pulled into a conversation (as often happens with parents, leaving children and their nannies to fend for themselves), Annie led them down an aisle until they were in front of the child-rearing section. She pointed triumphantly.

"The solution to my plight!"

Mary wrinkled her nose, folded her arms, and looked up at the ceiling.

Annie grabbed the box and tossed it at Mary.

"You carry it. It's yours."

Mary did not catch it. Instead, she turned and walked away, and the wet-alarm fell on top of Lord Tennyson's head.

"Oh, Tenny!" Pearl said, collapsing on him.

"Look what you did," Ezra said crossly to his sisters.

At once, they all swooped down to pet him and offer apologies. Lord Tennyson nodded, allowing their cooing, as he hoped it might soften their hearts to each other. But Mary's eyes immediately narrowed at her sister over his head. "I'm *not* carrying it and I'm *not* using it!"

Lord Tennyson picked up the box with his mouth and led the way to the cashier, Annie and Mary squabbling behind him.

"The wet-alarm is for your own good," Annie said. "If you don't stop wetting the bed, no one will marry you."

"Good!" Mary said. "I don't want to get married!"

"What's a wet-alarm?" Pearl said.

"An alarm that goes off when it gets wet," Annie said. "And maybe I'll finally get some sleep *and* be able to have friends over!"

"What friends?" Mary retorted.

Sweetums took that moment to swipe all the pacifiers off the hooks in the checkout aisle. This was not the improvement in her behavior Lord Tennyson was planning for, but he was glad for the distraction that paused the escalating fight between the sisters.

"It's not going to work," Ezra said, picking them up. "When she's really asleep, she doesn't wake up."

Mary shot him daggers with her eyes.

"I'm only trying to help," Ezra said, wanting to stay on Mary's good side.

Finally, Mr. McNiff joined them in line and began to sing from his musical.

"To dream, the impossible dream!"

"Dad," Annie said, glancing around her.

Mr. McNiff just smiled. "My dears, let me tell you a secret." He paused dramatically while they came closer. "I too was a bed wetter!"

The children wrinkled their noses, but Lord Tennyson inwardly applauded his forthrightness and attempt to soothe the building tension.

Still holding the box in his mouth, Lord Tennyson swung his head to the right, then to the left, and released. The wet-alarm flew into the air and landed upright on the revolving belt.

"Wow!" he heard the cashier say. Lord Tennyson bowed his head modestly.

But at that moment, Cal Hubbard arrived on the scene, dressed in his bright yellow Bellows Grocery uniform. Annie and Mary froze, looking at the conveyor belt. Lord Tennyson did too. He felt a pang of sympathy for red-faced

Mary, who was looking uncharacteristically unsure of herself, at the complete mercy of her older sister. He gulped, glancing impatiently at the cashier, who was talking to the customer in front of them about the weather instead of scanning and putting away the item.

This would be a crucial sister moment, one that could reverberate for good or ill among the siblings for months, or even years. Words could be forgiven, but they couldn't be unsaid.

"Hi, Cal," Annie said.

Cal nodded importantly, opening boxes and stacking rows of brightly colored packages of gum next to them. The stack was so big it was almost as tall as Cal.

"Hello, young man," Mr. McNiff said. "Good to see you working hard this summer."

"Yes, sir!" Cal said. "I'm building the letter *B* with the gum. It's taken me all morning to get this far."

"*B* for Bellows," Pearl said shyly.

"Exactly! What are you all doing here today?"

"Um . . . ," Annie began.

"We are buying a . . ." Pearl's voice became muffled as Mary clapped a hand over her mouth. Sweetums, sensing action and adventure, bounced up and down in her stroller.

Lord Tennyson anxiously growled under his breath to get the cashier's attention. "All right, all right, little fellow," she said, shaking her short blond hair and picking up the box.

But Lord Tennyson's relief was short-lived when the cashier announced, "A wet-alarm! My little sister had one of these. It worked, too."

"A what?" Cal asked.

"A wet-alarm!" Tate said. "For nighttime bed wetterth."

Pearl giggled through Mary's fingers.

Ezra looked away and pretended to be interested in a spaghetti-noodle sale.

"It's not for me," Annie said quickly.

"Well, it's not for me," Ezra said under his breath.

"She pees!" Sweetums yelled, just because she liked to yell.

"Shush!" Mary said, pulling on Sweetums's sprouting ponytail.

"AH!" Sweetums responded, whacking Mary.

Cal looked like he didn't want to talk about it anymore.

Mr. McNiff pulled out his wallet, exclaiming, "Forty-nine ninety-nine! Highway robbery is what it is."

When Cal glanced one more time between Annie and the wet-alarm, though, Annie couldn't help herself.

"IT'S FOR MARY," she burst out.

Lord Tennyson shook his head sadly, while Annie looked instantly guilty at her betrayal.

"No, it's for Annie!" Mary said immediately.

"Is not!"

"Is so!"

"Maybe it's for me!" Mr. McNiff said.

The children, Cal, and the cashier stared at him in horror.

Desperate to change the subject, Lord Tennyson stepped on Cal's foot and sniffed at the gum, his way of suggesting that Cal offer the children a piece. If they were chewing, they couldn't be fighting! Instead, Cal reached down to pet him, missing Lord Tennyson's *Give them gum!* signal entirely.

Mary looked like smoke was about to come out of her ears.

Lord Tennyson cocked his head at her. She cocked hers back at him, then looked at Annie's ponytail. Lord

Tennyson shook his head. *Mary McNiff, don't you dare!* She reached out her hand anyway.

Lord Tennyson stepped more forcefully on Cal's other foot. *GUM!*

Unfortunately, Lord Tennyson hadn't anticipated that with two paws on Cal's feet, he might somehow cause Cal to lose his balance.

"Whoa, whoa, whoa . . ." Cal stumbled back . . . right into the almost finished giant *B*.

As if in slow motion, hundreds of packages of gum came crumbling down on top of Cal.

The cashier screamed.

"Cal!" Annie yelled.

"Buried alive!" Pearl said woefully.

"In gum!" Tate said, impressed.

Sweetums clapped her hands at the show.

Lord Tennyson barked at the children to help Cal, and together they scrambled to unbury him. While Lord Tennyson was not impressed with Cal's lack of coordination, he *was* secretly impressed with his own ingenious use of distraction to keep the sisters from outright warfare in the grocery store.

Mr. Bellows was not so impressed, and the McNiffs were invited out of the grocery with a loud bellow of, "And get that dog out too!" Mortified, Lord Tennyson bolted. How had his excellent efforts gone so wrong, so soon?

Back in the car, the children chattered in excited voices for an entire mile before Mary remembered her sister's treachery.

"Traitor!" Mary hissed. "Mean, mean, mean."

"That's enough," Mr. McNiff began. "Let's pick up our new chicks."

"You have no family loyalty," Mary continued bitterly to Annie, but in a lower voice. "The Sibling Council is canceled. I have no allegiance to you anymore!" She folded her arms stubbornly, her short brown curls framing dark and stormy eyes.

"You can't declare it over!"

"I can, and I hate your guts," Mary said.

Oh dear. If she would only count to ten and breathe before she spat out venom, like Lord Tennyson had been teaching her.

"That's fine," Annie said back. "I detest your innards."

"Girls," Mr. McNiff warned again.

Lord Tennyson tried to remind each of the girls that the strength of the McNiff family was their love for one another. He pawed at Annie to prompt her to apologize, then put his head on Mary's arm as a way to soften her to it. His attempts went unheeded. Instead, he watched Mary's face turn to stone.

Alas, he feared that Naughty Mary was about to get *very* naughty.

The summer of getting his children to behave was off to a rather appalling start.

CHAPTER FOUR

Baby Chicks and Bunnies

THE TENSION BETWEEN THE TWO SISTERS WAS thicker than congealed pudding as the McNiff family drove from Bellows to Mr. Goody's farm. Mr. Goody lived just across the road from the McNiffs' pink farmhouse and had all sorts of animals that Lord Tennyson mostly stayed clear of, especially the terrifyingly large water buffalo. But it was not for this reason that Lord Tennyson stayed in the truck with Ezra, watching Mr. Goody open the barn door to where the new chicks were housed. No, the children didn't especially trust him around their chicks. He supposed this was fair, as his love of a good bird was well known, though he tried not to catch birds and eat them in front of the children because for some reason it upset them.

"More chickens," Ezra grumbled. "I wish we were getting a horse."

Lord Tennyson did not want a horse. He wanted chicken.

Alas, these birds were not for him. They would serve an important purpose in his child-training plan as they turned into large, feathery chickens that laid eggs for the family. Eventually, Lord Tennyson would help the children learn to gather their eggs, feed them, and clean out their coop—all without even *thinking* about eating the chickens himself. So, as he stood with his paws on the window, he tried to tamp down his giddiness at the prospect of chicks being in the house for six weeks.

He watched as the children stopped at the wooden fence just outside the barn to pet the three water buffalo, all named after great painters. (Mr. Goody liked to take a brush to paper after a long day's farmwork.) Mr. McNiff tiptoed across the driveway, trying to avoid getting cock-a-doodle-poo on his shiny shoes, and held his breath to avoid the scent of large bovine. Visits to animal farms always tried his patience. It was remarkable, really, that they lived in the country at all.

Ms. Monet, the mother buffalo, mooed loudly at the children, who scampered in delight.

"Baby Munch!" the children cooed at her baby. Ms. Monet took a step forward, standing protectively in front of her newborn.

Mr. Goody, who now lived alone except for his animals, smiled.

"It's okay, Ms. Monet. Good morning, McNiffs, my favorite neighborhood brood!"

Rembrandt, the new father and largest water buffalo, lifted his shiny black head. He looked past the children to Lord Tennyson, his eyes big, serious, and black as midnight. Lord Tennyson found himself shrinking into Ezra.

"All righty, then," Mr. Goody said. "Chicks are in here."

"Goody, goody, goody!" Tate said, clapping his hands and following Mr. Goody past a cage of bunnies and into the barn. Lord Tennyson peered after them as they disappeared from view. When he heard Sweetums's loud squeals, he hoped Annie was watching her, that she wasn't on the loose squeezing a chick too hard. Yesterday after the beach fiasco she had squeezed a banana with such roughness it had popped through the skin and slimed down her hands.

Ten minutes later, Mr. McNiff and the children emerged with a small brown box, looking as happy as if it were Christmas morning. Lord Tennyson exhaled with relief. The chicks were still alive. Sitting in that small brown box. He inhaled deeply, anticipating their lovely scent.

"Water, chick feed, and a heat lamp is all they need for the next six weeks," Mr. Goody said. "Keep 'em away from the dog, too." He jutted his chin toward Lord Tennyson, who pulled in his tongue and attempted to look stoic and still.

He was not *just* a dog. He could control himself.

Meanwhile, Pearl and Tate stopped to pet the two giant bunnies.

"They're adorable!" Tate said, looking especially smitten with the large brown bunny with large brown eyes. "I've alwayth wanted a North American porcupine, but they're very rare. Can we have her inthtead? What'th her name?"

"I don't name 'em," Mr. Goody said. "They're not for sale. I . . ." He glanced uneasily at Mr. McNiff.

"We're here for chicks," Mr. McNiff reminded them quickly.

"Two-fifty apiece, plus some chick feed, comes to thirty dollars," Mr. Goody said.

But Tate and Pearl were smitten. The bunnies sniffed Pearl's hand and she giggled as she begged, "Oh please, Daddy."

"Bunny!" Sweetums shrieked.

The hopeful look on Pearl's face was so earnest it could break your heart. Of all the McNiff children, it was she Lord Tennyson was the most protective of. Pearl was one of those especially gentle, sweet souls whose feelings were easily crushed.

Mr. Goody shook his head. "Uh, they won't be here for long." Dressed in his blue overalls and old brown work boots, he pulled his hat down slightly over his bushy eyebrows.

"Time to go," Mr. McNiff said, hastily handing over the money.

Pearl stepped closer to the bunny cage.

Lord Tennyson sensed meltdown mode.

"Come on, Pearl," Annie said, sensing it too. "Mary, help me."

Despite the drama at Bellows, together they tried to coax Pearl and Tate toward the truck. (Lord Tennyson was momentarily hopeful that a future Naughty Mary attack might be averted.)

But Pearl didn't move. Shyly, she asked, "Where are they going?"

There was a long silence.

Mr. Goody didn't believe in sugarcoating farm life, but looking at Pearl, he couldn't seem to say anything more about the bunnies.

"Rabbit stew," Ezra said from the truck. Unfortunately, his voice traveled well.

"Come on, Pearl girl!" Mary said, pulling on her sister's hand.

Instead of moving, Pearl let out a bloodcurdling scream.

Annie and Mary tried to carry her to the truck, the brown box moving up into the air and back down as Mary juggled her squirming sister and the chicks all the way.

"Save the bunnies!" Pearl cried.

Lord Tennyson was normally very attuned to meltdowns

and catastrophes and how to comfort Pearl, but the chicks were getting closer and he suddenly could not take his eyes off the box.

Ezra helped lift Pearl into the truck, leaving the chicks unattended in the front seat. There was a peep and a rustling inside. Lord Tennyson sniffed and took a step forward. *No! I mustn't!* Employing his incredible willpower, he turned away from the birds to see Pearl weeping uncontrollably. He began licking her tearstained cheeks.

"Save the bunnies!" she cried. *"PLEASE!"*

"Pearl," Mr. McNiff said, looking conflicted as he started the truck and drove slowly down the road, away from Mr. Goody's farm. "You know that this is what happens on a farm."

"Rabbit meat is actually pretty good," Ezra said. "We had it at camp. Remember, Dad?"

"Ezra, stop!" Mary yelled. "This is all your fault!"

"But it's true. . . ."

"Seriously," Annie said. "You didn't have to say anything, you bigmouth."

Ezra's whole body deflated at the criticism.

"Bunny?" Sweetums asked.

Pearl began to wail again, and this time Tate joined her, putting his arms protectively around her. "Dad!" Tate shouted. "THAVE THE BUNNIETH!"

Mr. McNiff closed his eyes. "Oh, for heaven's sake."

Ten minutes later, Lord Tennyson was sitting in the back seat, held in place by Ezra, who had two fingers wrapped around his collar. Lord Tennyson had not forgotten the chicks, but this was quite unnecessary. He was in control of himself and instead sat staring at the two large bunnies on Pearl's lap. Pearl had stopped crying. She should have looked pleased. Instead, she looked terrified.

"They have long nails," Pearl whispered.

This was the thing about children. They never seemed to want what they so desperately wanted a mere two seconds ago once they got it.

"Hold them tight," Mr. McNiff instructed.

"Don't let them hop out the window," Mary added.

"Or let them eat your fingers," Ezra said.

"Let's name them Felicity and Delilah," Annie suggested.

"I like Pinkie," Tate said, stroking the brown bunny.

"That's a silly name," Ezra said. "How about Rocky?"

"If I can name them, you can play in my room for five minutes every day, all week," Annie said.

"It's *our* room," Mary said.

As they drove, Mr. McNiff frowned and sniffed like Lord Tennyson. They had many things in common, their exceptional sense of smell being one of them.

"They have a particular . . . aroma I cannot abide," he said. Here, Lord Tennyson disagreed. He reveled in their scent.

Mr. McNiff pulled into the driveway, where their pink house stood majestically up against the tall pine trees. The fields were cornflower yellow, the tall grasses nearly long enough to hay in a few short weeks.

Mr. McNiff smiled and looked up at the house. "I might be a city man, but I do enjoy our pink country retreat. Even with these six noisy children, my terrific mate here . . ." He paused to rub Lord Tennyson's ears. "And now two bunnies and six baby chicks."

Lord Tennyson beamed.

Once inside, he excitedly ran laps around the kitchen table, where the six new chicks now sat in their large box filled with wood shavings, special chick food, a small bowl of water, and a heat lamp.

Honey smiled but wagged her finger at Lord Tennyson. "No getting on the table."

Hmph! As if Lord Tennyson *ever* stood on the kitchen table.

The children cooed and clucked as they petted the chicks.

Lord Tennyson remembered his puppy days, surrounded by these same squealing children who were instantly smitten by his cuteness. Mr. McNiff, the great mister of the house, had named him Lord Tennyson, after his favorite poet, a fitting name for such a dignified miniature schnauzer. On their first meeting, the rowdy children had nearly smothered him with love, and it was then that Lord Tennyson had known his true calling in life: raising the McNiff children. He hadn't known it would extend to welcoming so many animals, too, but oh, this morning he did not mind.

The chicks were lovely, with soft yellow fluff and tiny pecking beaks. He would love to hop on the table just for one peek, maybe a little sniff . . . but no! Lord Tennyson did *not* climb up on tables. Instead, he watched as Sweet-ums crawled laps around the kitchen floor, following the hopping bunnies. He was momentarily distracted by the bunnies, but he had already sniffed them and decided they were too large to chase. Also, they had very sharp nails, and Mr. Goody had warned about their razor-sharp teeth. He would have to watch the baby closely.

"That's Edith," Annie said, excitedly showing Honey the chicks. "And this is Lady Mary, Sybil, Anna, Mrs. Pat-more, and Lavinia!"

"They're darling," Honey said.

Annie and Mary might have had a chance of reconcili-ation over the chicks if Honey had not followed up with, "And did you get the other item?"

Oh dear.

Annie, regret forgotten, heartlessly tossed Mary the wet-alarm and said, "The sheets are in the dryer. You can make the bed."

Lord Tennyson followed Mary as she stomped upstairs instead and flung herself onto the unmade bed.

He sighed alongside her, letting Mary know he under-stood life was sometimes hard with older sisters.

Mary sat up and smiled. He smiled back.

But when Mary began to sing, Lord Tennyson quickly realized that he had not effectively convinced Mary to ascend to a more benevolent state of being.

"We're going to have to retaliate, retaliate, retaliate," Mary sang. "We're going to have to retaliate against that MEAN GIRL!"

Mary jumped off the bed but stopped singing at the sight of the large yellow circle on the mattress.

"Come on, Tenny," Mary said. "Let's push the mattress to the window to dry."

Mary pushed and he pulled. The mattress was heavy, but Lord Tennyson could tell it was the heavy weight of that spot that Mary was really carrying.

"It's not like I *mean* to wet the bed," Mary said. "It's just so hard to wake up."

He nodded sympathetically.

"And also, Tenny . . ." She paused and bit her lip. "I'm going to swim camp in a few weeks, and . . . I can't wet the bed at camp!"

Mary was right, and she certainly couldn't bring the wet-alarm without feeling embarrassed.

Just when Lord Tennyson thought Mary's worries had distracted her from plotting revenge, the key to it appeared. A literal one.

Mary suddenly stopped and gaped. Lord Tennyson followed her eyes. There, sitting on the box spring, was a small key.

The key to Annie's locked safe.

And both he and Mary knew that inside Annie's locked safe was her diary.

Oh no.

CHAPTER FIVE

Annie's Secrets

LORD TENNYSON DID WHAT HE HAD TO: HE JUMPED onto the box spring and sat on the key.

Mary pushed him gently.

"Come on, Tenny."

But he sat firm and shook his head at her.

Her mouth twitched. "Tenny . . ."

Drop it, he growled.

Soon they were in a wrestling match, rolling over

until—*ow!* His old knees were beyond wrestling with an eleven-year-old.

Mary triumphantly held up the key.

She didn't hesitate to find and unlock the safe under the bed, take out the diary, and begin reading her sister's secrets.

He watched disapprovingly, but Mary just looked up and smiled wickedly.

When she felt Lord Tennyson's insistent gaze too keenly, she held the diary up in front of her face so she couldn't see him looking at her.

Meanwhile, Mr. McNiff's voice echoed through the floor.

"There are animals *everywhere.* There are even chickens on the *kitchen table.* Are they *pooping* up there? We can never eat here again! In fact, I've lost my appetite!" Clearly, Mr. McNiff's affection for the newest members of their family was waning rapidly.

Mary looked up from the diary, giggling at her father's dramatics.

Lord Tennyson let her pull him to her lap, but he refused to let her off the hook, pawing at the open book to say, *Get that diary back into the locked safe!*

"Mary!"

Both Mary and Lord Tennyson jumped, and the diary fell to the floor. Together they peered out the window to see Ezra dribbling the basketball across the driveway and driving for a layup.

"I need someone to play with!" Ezra hollered. He was always more content during the school months, when there were sports teams to be on and friends to play with. But as they lived outside the town, unlike their friends, and had no other children on the street, it usually fell to the McNiff siblings to entertain one another.

Mary, who clearly wanted to continue reading the diary, seemed to be casting about for an excuse, but it was Mr. McNiff who stepped outside. Knowing his mister was not a sports man himself, Lord Tennyson was proud of the sacrifice he was making. Mr. McNiff carefully unbuttoned the sleeves of his pink pinstriped dress shirt and rolled them up.

"Son," he said. "I'll do my best."

Ezra looked skeptical. "Mary!" he yelled. "Um, Dad needs you!"

"I'm cleaning my room," she yelled back.

Ezra looked *very* confused. Mary *never* voluntarily cleaned her room.

Now that she'd said it, Lord Tennyson was going to hold her to it. He looked at the bed and back to Mary.

"Fine," she growled. "Let's . . . clean the room."

Lord Tennyson helped her push and pull the mattress back on top of the box spring. Then Mary sprayed bleach onto it until the smell was gone and the yellow stain was a blotchy white. Next came the clean sheets, comforter, and pillows, which Lord Tennyson plumped himself.

"Won't Annie be so surprised!" Mary crowed—as if he didn't know she had other motives!

There was nothing Mary could have done that was more suspicious than cleaning and making the bed with a smile on her face. But what was she planning?

And what had Annie been thinking with her choice of hiding places for the key—especially when the sister she shared a room with was Mary? Didn't she know that mattresses were entirely too obvious? Annie had probably read it in one of her novels. Then again, when you shared a room, there were very few true hiding places.

While Ezra once again explained to Mr. McNiff how

to catch a basketball, Lord Tennyson saw an opportunity to redeem himself. When Mary reached down for the diary, he stood on it.

"Tenny," she whispered. "Let go and I'll read you the best parts."

Lord Tennyson shook his head. Admittedly, he was curious. After all, Annie was his oldest child, paving the way for the others. But he could not. It was a complete invasion of privacy.

"I'll put it away, then."

As soon as Lord Tennyson relented, Mary snatched the book and began to read anyway.

Dear Diary,

I'm really not one of those boy-crazy girls, but I think about Cal Hubbard all the time!!!! The thing is, we've always been friends and now it's, like, weird between us. I can't even say hi without feeling so awkward!

I wonder if he's in love with me. Or am I in love with him? Is this what love is?

"And then," Mary said, peering wickedly into Lord Tennyson's eyes . . .

Annie McNiff Hubbard

Annie Louise Hubbard

Do you think people will call me Old Mother Hubbard?

Mary fell to the ground laughing. "*I'll* definitely call her that!"

Lord Tennyson remained as solemn as a stone, processing this confirmation of the burgeoning crush between his eldest child and the grocery boy.

"The best part is next, though. 'True Love, by Annie McNiff,'" Mary said. "It's a poem. A really, really bad poem."

When I'm lonely or feeling sad,
I think of you and then I'm glad.
When my heart skips a beat,
I feel a warm glow
That we're together
Through every
High and every low.

Lord Tennyson covered his eyes with his paw for a moment. Though he disagreed with Mary's wickedness, he was almost glad to hear the poem, glad to know what they were up against: boys.

Was this normal teenage-girl behavior? Annie was the

oldest, and that meant she was always the first to do every-thing. This was uncharted territory for him, and he briefly wondered if he was up to this particular task. Some days, Lord Tennyson wished he had someone to consult regard-ing teenage girls, but not on his life would he engage with Fat Cat on the matter.

Lord Tennyson and Mary were so engrossed in her reading that they did not hear the footsteps coming up the stairs until they were right outside the bedroom door. Mary leaped up and sat on top of the diary just as the door opened.

"Oh, hi there, Annie!" Mary said.

Annie paused and looked at her unusually pink-cheeked, cheerful sister. Her eyes narrowed in suspicion.

Behind Annie, Pearl, Tate, and Sweetums rushed in. They were all wearing long dress-up capes, even Annie, who, in addition to her cape, wore a crown.

With the arrival of her subjects, Annie strode forward, her chin in the air. So enthralled was she with being queen, she forgot the color of Mary's cheeks and the guilty look on her face.

Lord Tennyson looked at the open bedroom door,

knowing that the chicks were on the kitchen table, unattended. He swallowed. This was no time to get distracted.

"Tenny boy," Pearl crooned, coming close to him, tutu in hand.

Oh no. Not this again.

And yet, because Lord Tennyson knew the virtue of patience and wanted to avert all-out war between Annie and Mary, he stood still while Tate and Pearl wrestled the pink sparkly tutu onto him. He looked down at himself and sighed. Mary tapped her foot nervously.

Annie suddenly stopped walking and stared at the bed.

Lord Tennyson gulped. Did Annie suspect Mary had the diary? Was in fact *sitting* on it?

"You made the bed!" Annie exclaimed in an English accent while tossing her cape. "How very lovely."

Lord Tennyson peeked over at Mary with relief.

Annie sniffed the air for a lingering bed-wetting smell.

Mary scowled and Lord Tennyson's relief evaporated.

"Royal subject," Annie said. "I'll forgive you this once."

"Shut it, queen!" Mary said, refusing the olive branch.

"OW!" they heard from outside. Lord Tennyson

scrambled to join the five siblings peering out the window at the driveway, where Mr. McNiff was holding his nose.

"Oh, Daddy," Pearl cried.

Mr. McNiff straightened. "I'm . . . bleeding! I'm bleeding, for heaven's sake. What kind of game is this? It's a brutal bloodbath."

"Sorry, Dad," Ezra said. "But you have to hold out your hands when someone throws you the ball." He looked up at the window again. "Mary!"

Lord Tennyson wanted to assist Mr. McNiff, but he couldn't leave Mary in her troubles. In addition, he was still in a sparkly tutu. With Annie looking out the window, Mary made her move, sliding off the windowsill, diary in hand. Well, almost. The diary slipped from her hand, making a loud thwack onto the floor right in front of Lord Tennyson's nose. With horror, he noticed bite marks from when he and Mary had tugged it back and forth. He would look like an accomplice!

"Mary!"

Annie whirled around from the window just as he leaped upon the book and collapsed atop it. Now he really *was* an accomplice!

"What?" Mary asked, eyes wide.

"Play with us? Don't be mad anymore."

"I'm not."

Annie's eyes narrowed. "What are you doing up here all alone and acting all weird, then?"

"Cleaning, duh."

Lord Tennyson looked from one sister to another. Mary was being naughty, yes, but he also remembered the hurt look on her face in Bellows, the worry in her eyes when they'd returned home, and how he was her one true confidant regarding camp and bed-wetting. With a swift flick of his paw, the diary flew under the bed while he ran around the room, his pink tutu flying behind him. The children began to laugh.

"Tenny boy!"

"Oh, you're so cute!"

"Tutu!" Sweetums said, putting her head down and crawling fast after him, knocking into the shoe rack along the way and sending shoes everywhere. It reminded him once again that he had to get that baby to walk.

Pearl and Tate climbed up onto the bed and started to jump.

"No jumping on my bed!" Annie exclaimed. "And that mattress has pee on it."

Mary's anger was again ignited as Pearl and Tate quickly jumped off.

"Get out!" she said.

"I wasn't being mean, just stating a fact," Annie said.

"Well, it *was* mean!"

"Fine," Annie said, motioning for her subjects to follow. "I'll just go play with *my* chicks and royal subjects downstairs!"

Pearl and Tate followed Annie out the door.

Sweetums emerged from the pile of shoes with an unearthed pacifier she had long ago lost. It had hair and dust and carpet fuzz on it. She popped it into her mouth and chewed contentedly, crawling out the door after her siblings. Lord Tennyson sighed. It had taken a good month for him to train her to sleep without it. He had even sacrificed his beard for her to chew on when she was especially crabby.

With Sweetums gone, Mary grabbed the diary and, to his relief, dropped it into the safe once again.

"Thank you, Tenny," she said. "I couldn't have done it without you."

He was entirely unsure that was a good thing, and he was not often unsure.

Lord Tennyson wanted to sit Mary down for a talking-to, but she stuck out her tongue at Annie's side of the bed before flouncing downstairs. He could hear the arguing start all over again from where he stood in the middle of the bedroom, still wearing the sparkly pink tutu.

"Better watch yourself," he heard Mary say. "I *know* things you don't want me to know!"

Lord Tennyson stood still, hoping Honey was out in her garden and not witnessing more arguing on his watch. He had hoped to stop their fighting from escalating, but now he wondered—had he made things better or far worse?

CHAPTER SIX

Of Chores and Snakes

AFTER A RESTLESS SLEEP, PONDERING ONE DILEMMA, Lord Tennyson walked downstairs with Mr. McNiff to encounter another. Together they surveyed the kitchen.

Lord Tennyson had left the children alone for a mere ten minutes, and now a gallon of milk sat on the counter, warming in the sunlight, the top left off. Drops of milk dribbled from it onto dirty dishes piled in the sink. A happy fly buzzed around the remains of toast and jam.

Clean dishes were still in the dishwasher from the night before, waiting to be put away. Cupboards were open, drawers pulled out. Cereal boxes and crumbs littered the counters, the floor, and the table. Even Honey's new chemistry experiment—something she called "sourdough"—had bubbled over out of its glass jar onto the counter. Lord Tennyson looked at Mr. McNiff. They frowned in agreement.

As a breeze blew in from the open window, they both sniffed. Whereas Lord Tennyson loved the smell of any kind of manure, Mr. McNiff shuddered and plugged his nose.

"*When* are those creatures leaving this kitchen?"

Lord Tennyson hoped it was never.

As if on cue, one of the chicks flapped its wings so hard that it flew right out of the box and onto the kitchen table!

Lord Tennyson froze with quivering excitement, his eyes tracking each movement.

Mr. McNiff gasped, put his hands out, and said, "Steady, boy, I got it." He tiptoed closer and closer to the table, reaching . . . but the bird flew into the air.

"Ah!" Mr. McNiff yelled, chasing after it, hands outstretched. The chicken flew again and quickly landed, perching atop the hanging light fixture, making it swing.

Mr. McNiff chased the chicken again and again, getting close every time, but not quite able to simply *grab* it. It was so entertaining that Lord Tennyson briefly forgot how easy it would be to show Mr. McNiff how to do it.

Mr. McNiff circled the kitchen table several times until finally he lunged and caught the chick with both hands. "Got it!" Mr. McNiff yelled, his voice trembling slightly as he held out the chick. "Look at that—AHHHH!" The chick flapped wildly, and Mr. McNiff flung it into the direction of the box, where it landed safely inside on the wood shavings. Lord Tennyson's heart swelled with pride. How clever and capable his mister was! He swallowed, wondering if Mr. McNiff was also thinking of chicken dinner.

Mr. McNiff closed his eyes and held his heart. "The whole house is a land mine of messes and near-disastrous ends."

Lord Tennyson was used to these types of McNiff messes and disasters, but every summer when everyone was home all day long, Mr. McNiff was caught by surprise.

"We've created monsters," Mr. McNiff said, looking at his children, who were actually relatively tame for once, lazily strewn about the kitchen and living room. Lord

Tennyson wanted to point out that the children were all reading—and that was a win. But his heart nearly stopped at the smug look of glee on Mary's face as she read the large open dictionary on her lap, something he'd never seen her read before, especially during summer vacation. Surely there wasn't a *stolen diary* tucked behind it?

Before he could investigate, he heard a loud squawk. Sweetums had managed to climb atop the kitchen table next to the new chicks, wearing nothing but her morning cereal. Mr. McNiff looked out the window and saw his wife, Honey.

"I suddenly understand why she spends so much time in the garden." He looked down at Lord Tennyson. "Old boy, we've got work to do. Maybe too much."

Lord Tennyson gave Mr. McNiff a curt nod, but the "too much" rang in his ears. He wished he could tell Mr. McNiff how hard he was working and thinking on this subject. After all, it took time to see progress when raising children.

And "old boy." It was a term of affection, wasn't it?

Looking down at his once-dark fur (which was now more salt-and-pepper in color), he was caught by surprise.

When had he had time to grow so old? He immediately dismissed the implication of his white hairs. He might look old, and his knees might hurt, but with age came wisdom and a robust spirit, did it not?

But then Mr. McNiff tipped his head and muttered something under his breath that sent alarm bells through Lord Tennyson's head. Something that sounded like ". . . *more help around here.*"

His brow furrowed and he looked up at Mr. McNiff, who patted his head, almost apologetically.

"Savagery," Mr. McNiff said loudly in the direction of the living room, where the rest of the children sat. "Complete savagery!"

Lord Tennyson barked for their attention with a determination to show Mr. McNiff his great competence.

"What's up with you, Dad?" Ezra asked.

"Children," Mr. McNiff said, "I have an important rehearsal this morning."

"Cool, can I go into town with you and meet Megan?" Annie asked, looking up from a book.

"If the house didn't look like a dumpster, I'd be inclined to say yes."

"It's not my mess!" Annie said.

"Are you working on your play today?" Mary asked, wanting to change the subject from housecleaning.

"Yes, the part where Cervantes has been thrown into the dungeon—which is exactly what will happen to all of you if you don't clean up this mess immediately!"

"Dungeonth!" Tate said excitedly. "Dungeonth are cold and dark and have thkweaky little mithe."

Pearl shrieked, prompting Tate to change his tune from excited to scared.

Lord Tennyson thought he might like dungeons if he could chase squeaky little mice.

Mr. McNiff nodded down at Lord Tennyson, as if making an agreement among men, then set off.

Lord Tennyson nodded back and faced the children. By the time Mr. McNiff returned home, there would be no need to ever think the words "more help" again.

When Ezra tried to leave the kitchen, Lord Tennyson blocked his way.

When Mary dropped her bowl in the sink without rinsing it or putting it in the dishwasher, he growled.

When Sweetums got filthy crawling across the floor,

he licked her off using water from his own dog dish while also nudging her to a standing position, a reminder that hands could put things away, not just crawl. She answered by pulling on his ears.

At least when Lord Tennyson picked up a wet rag and trotted over to Pearl, she dutifully took it and began washing the kitchen floor. Tate began to help her. Lord Tennyson nodded his approval.

Still, there was arguing.

"It's summer vacation," Mary complained. "It's always a mess, Tenny. You know that."

"I told Megan I'd meet her today," Annie whined.

"It'th too hot, Tenny," said Tate as he scrubbed. "Right, Pearl?"

Pearl looked anxiously to Lord Tennyson, who stood his ground.

"Let's hurry up, then," Ezra said irritably.

With his insistence, the children began at least making a half-hearted effort at cleaning.

Well, all except one.

"Do something, Mary!" Annie said.

"You're not the boss of me!" Mary retorted, kicking the

Tupperware full of brown sugar across the floor. Unfortunately, the lid was loose. Brown sugar exploded all over the kitchen floor.

"Mary!" came the chorus of siblings.

Sweetums crawled as fast as she could, sugar getting stuck to her knees and hands and her whole body as she licked the floor, reminding Lord Tennyson of Fat Cat. He shuddered, while also fearing he had taught her this form of bathing mere minutes ago.

Sweetums grinned. "Yum!"

"Look, Pearl," Tate said, lighting the gas stove. "Fire!"

Lord Tennyson leaped over to Tate and barked with furrowed eyebrows, but it wasn't until Pearl yelled that Tate turned the stove off. Lord Tennyson made note of it for this summer's training. The two of them were entirely too codependent and must learn to use their own wee brains or listen to others before the old farmhouse went up in flames!

In the end, the kitchen wasn't spotless; one could find small crumbs in corners, and there were multiple sticky spots under the table, but it *was* a vast improvement. Lord Tennyson hoped Mr. McNiff and Honey would be pleased and appeased. Finally released by Lord Tennyson, Annie escaped to her room. Over the last week, Mary hadn't dared enter without Lord Tennyson's protection, though he hadn't seen her with the diary. Maybe she really had been reading the dictionary and he could give himself a pat on the back. Cheered by a somewhat successful morning, he allowed himself just a moment to sniff the chick smell.

He could feel the drool coming, priming him to eat.

Pearl gingerly touched a chick with her finger before pulling it back. "They're getting so big."

"Don't be a fraidy-cat," Mary said, coming over to hold him. "Just catch one." Oh, how he wished she were talking to him.

Pearl slowly put both hands in the box, but as soon as the chicks moved, she shrieked and pulled her hands back out, causing Tate to do the same, though he seemed more fascinated by the chicks than scared. "I can't!" she wailed.

Lord Tennyson had an idea. He nudged open a kitchen drawer with his nose and pulled out a pair of mismatched hot-pad gloves with his teeth. He trotted back to the table and dropped them in front of Pearl.

Mary laughed. "We're not going to cook them!"

As wonderful as that sounded, this was not his intent. He looked at Pearl and back to the gloves.

"Good idea, Tenny!" Tate whispered, his eyes big behind his red glasses as he handed the gloves to Pearl.

Pearl slid them on her hands and held them up. *Yes, that's right.* She bit her lip, reached into the box, and easily caught a chick.

"I did it!" Pearl yelled. Tate clapped, and Mary nodded admiringly.

Lord Tennyson beamed, then bowed his head. With such genius ideas, he often had to remind himself of the virtue of modesty.

"Adorable!" Pearl said, holding Edith tightly.

"They're getting bigger," Mary said. "Look!" She put the yellow chick named Sybil on the floor, three feet away from Lord Tennyson. She giggled, knowing exactly how to tease him in the worst way. He could smell the chick acutely now. Sybil flicked her head left, eyed him with her beady eye, and then pecked the kitchen floor. He gulped, willing himself not to open his mouth, not to be overcome by the scent. *But oh, wouldn't it be fun to catch a chick just like Mr. McNiff had?* He took a step forward.

"No . . . ," Mary warned.

Luckily for Sybil *and* Mary, the back door opened and Ezra called for him, shaking him out of his trance.

"Tenny! Let's play!"

Lord Tennyson gave a regretful look at the delicious bird but consoled himself with how impressed Mr. McNiff would be with his self-control.

After shaking off the initial stiffness, he was soon running across the grass chasing Ezra—one of the very best parts of his job! After a while he lay down in the shade to rest, Ezra by his side. He dozed until Ezra suddenly startled. Lord Tennyson did the same, then jumped to his feet. Both of them stared at a small twisting movement in the green grass. A snake!

It was a small garter, long and black with colorful weaving down the back.

"No!" Ezra whispered when Lord Tennyson pounced and pawed at it. He barked twice but relented. The snake curled sharply around Ezra's fingers.

"Snake!" he said, holding it up in the air triumphantly.

At that moment, Tate came over, followed by a crawling Sweetums.

"Whoa," Tate said. Sweetums hissed, "Ssssss," as the creature poked out its small forked tongue.

"Thlithery thneaky thnakey," Tate said, tiptoeing closer. "Thnaketh are reptileth. They're cold-blooded, legleth, and carnivorouth." Lord Tennyson nodded, proud of Tate's ability to keep a million animal facts in his head.

Ezra smiled and looked toward the house. "Wouldn't our sisters like to see our cold-blooded, legless, carnivorous reptile?"

Tate's eyes lit up and he held out his hands, but then he paused.

"Ooooh, I jutht love thnaketh . . . but Pearl ith thcared. Ethra . . ."

Ezra laughed wickedly, sounding a little too much like his older sister.

Lord Tennyson closed his eyes. Never a moment's peace with these children.

Despite all Lord Tennyson's good work that morning and his repeated gestures for Ezra to leave the snake outside, his oldest boy couldn't resist the reaction he knew he would get showing it to his sisters.

"Look what I found," Ezra said casually, coming in through the back door.

Lord Tennyson braced himself.

"What is it?" Annie asked, coming down the stairs.

"Ah, just a . . . snake." He held it up, letting it dangle from his hand.

Lord Tennyson's heart sank at the most unfortunate timing because just at that moment Mr. McNiff walked in through the front door after his rehearsal. What happened next can only be described as a complete breakdown.

Mr. McNiff let out a terrified yelp.

Annie screeched so loudly it made Lord Tennyson's ears hurt: "AAAAAAAAAAAAAAAHHHHHHH-HHHHHHH!"

She jumped onto the counter just as Mr. McNiff did the same.

Mary laughed, delighted by her sister's reaction, and made fun of her shriek.

Sweetums screamed happily because everyone else was screaming.

And Pearl cried and tried to jump onto the counter too, but she got stuck halfway up and dropped her precious Nicholas onto the floor.

"Nicholas! Save my Nicholas from the snake!" she

sobbed, looking to Tate for help, but he was too enraptured with the snake to move.

Honey rushed in the back door. "What in the world?"

"It'th a therpent!" Tate yelled over the screaming. "They can be dithtinguished from legleth lithardth by their lack of eyelidth and ekthternal earth."

"I don't care, Tate!" Annie yelled. "Get it out of the house!"

Instead, Ezra put the snake on the floor. It lay motionless as more screams echoed from wall to wall. Then it darted left, and Lord Tennyson, who had been at the ready, determined not to let it undo all the good he'd accomplished that day, pounced with one paw. The snake swiveled and curled under him. Lord Tennyson sniffed it, pleased with his quick reflexes, then let the snake go, ready to do it again in case Mr. McNiff or Honey had not seen his spectacular defense of the family.

"Get it, Tenny, get it!" Annie yelled.

"NOOOO!" Ezra yelled, lunging for Lord Tennyson.

"He'th going to eat it like a hot dog," Tate said, beginning to cry. "Hot dogth are my motht favorite food!"

"Outside!" Mr. McNiff managed to eke out. "Ezra— OUT!"

"Geez, Dad, it's just a snake!"

"Out!"

Ezra wrestled Lord Tennyson for the snake as they went out the back door. But he didn't let the slithering creature go.

"I'm going to keep it for my very own pet," Ezra whispered. "Oh, don't worry, you're still my favorite, Tenny. It's just that I have to share you with everyone. It'll be nice to have something that's just mine, you know?" He stroked the snake. "Look at how cool its skin is."

Lord Tennyson sympathized. He knew Ezra always got caught in the middle of his sisters and rarely got to pick the activity or have a say in the Sibling Council. Still . . .

Ezra looked up to his bedroom window. "We'll have to sneak it in. Don't tell, okay?" Lord Tennyson rubbed his eyes and chewed on his paws. If he had a piece of kibble for every secret he was supposed to keep, he would be extremely well fed. How difficult it was to be loyal to each member of the family when their goals were so misaligned! The house hadn't gone up in flames and the children were alive, but sadly, Mr. McNiff and Honey had only witnessed the utter mayhem, not the newly tidy kitchen and peaceful hours prior!

Then, as if to make matters worse, from out of the corner of his eye Lord Tennyson saw a shadow duck behind a pine tree before leaping onto the long white McNiff fence.

Fat Cat tiptoed along it, looking like a giant white cotton ball.

Fat Cat lived a *very* pampered life down the street with Mrs. Gage. She had zero responsibility and spent her time eavesdropping and lying in undignified positions for a tummy scratch. Lord Tennyson thought her a complete waste of hair. Besides, Mr. McNiff was allergic to cats—all the more reason to hold a grudge against her.

She meowed noisily and was soon followed by her feline cousins, Widdy Boo and Nuff, whom he didn't mind especially. It was the smug Fat Cat who had a knack for showing up whenever there was trouble. Together, the cat parade strutted as if to mock his pain. The last thing he needed was criticism from that hairy, show-offy spy who was not relied upon to raise any children at all!

As Ezra snuck back into the house and upstairs, Lord Tennyson ignored the cats and burrowed under the porch for a quick strategizing session that only *looked* like a dog nap.

CHAPTER SEVEN

The Sibling Council

FOR TWO WEEKS, LORD TENNYSON NUDGED MARY AT least twice in the dark of night to get up, before the wet-alarm could do it for him. She was motivated too, fearful that if the alarm sounded as it had the very first night, the whole family would come running again—a mortifying scenario that had done nothing to heal the rift between the sisters. He was exhausted after so many sleepless nights, but his excellent effort was paying off. Mary had woken up dry for six nights straight, and, delighted with her progress, kissed him forty-three consecutive times on the head. She declared herself cured and ready to go to swim camp after all.

"I'm so glad my solution worked," Annie said, taking credit for curing Mary.

"What? The only thing you deserve credit for is embarrassing me!" Mary said.

They were both sent to their shared room for arguing and had spent the last thirty minutes in a frosty silence. Lord Tennyson wished Annie would stop antagonizing Mary, thinking of the diary. Mary's focus on fixing her problem seemed to have stalled her retaliation, but Lord Tennyson knew she had not forgotten. He trotted back and forth between the two of them, trying to coax them into a peaceful, sisterly truce.

Ezra peeked his head in several times before fully entering. After Lord Tennyson had checked all his pockets for snake contraband, Ezra plopped himself on the bed.

"Are you done being mad?"

Mary giggled while she once again read behind the ridiculously large dictionary, which confirmed Lord

Tennyson's suspicions. It was both a miracle and a reckless maneuver that Mary still had the safe key and Annie had not discovered it missing.

"As if we really think you're so smart reading the dictionary," Annie said, rolling her eyes.

"Oh, I'm smart," Mary said. "And I *am* reading."

Ezra looked from one sister to another, not daring to side with either one.

"Really," Annie stated. "Tell us what word you're reading about, then."

"Revenge," Mary said. "To avenge oneself after a terrible, horrible, no good, very bad wrong has been committed against you."

Annie just laughed. "I knew it," she said. "She's just reading an Alexander picture book."

"I love that book!" Ezra said.

"See also Retaliation. Retribution," Mary continued. She growled the last word: "VENGEANCE."

Annie looked partially frightened for a second before snorting. "Mary McNiff, you'll never get the best of me."

Lord Tennyson wished he could muzzle both of them and do the talking.

A slow smile spread across Mary's face, and a tiny corner of a smaller book slid out from behind the dictionary.

Annie didn't see, but Ezra's mouth dropped open into a horrified, silent O.

Ezra didn't say a word, but for the rest of the day Lord Tennyson could see him stewing. He idolized Mary, but even he knew reading a diary was too far. How much loyalty should one extend, even to one's sibling?

Neither Annie nor Mary had called a Sibling Council for weeks, despite Annie's initial threat. Ezra wanted to call a Sibling Council, but he wasn't accustomed to being in charge with two older sisters, or having his opinion heard, and did not act on Lord Tennyson's subtle encouragement.

Without intervention, Lord Tennyson worried that the children would only become further estranged. Honey was so enraptured with the garden and that sourdough creature on the counter, and Mr. McNiff so busy directing a musical, that they were hardly aware of the growing rift between the children. Lord Tennyson was somewhat relieved, as further division did not help his case about that whole "real nanny" business, but oh, the emotional loads he carried!

The children needed to be reminded of their one true pack: each other.

So Lord Tennyson changed tactics. To prompt Ezra to call a Council, Lord Tennyson would have to perform a treacherous act, one he felt bad about, but that he hoped would avoid a worse conflict if Mary were to act on her ideas of revenge. Very early one morning, he stuck his paw under the girls' mattress, pulled out the key, and let it fall onto the bedroom rug.

Annie discovered it almost immediately.

"Mary!" she said, holding it up in the air.

"Wasn't me," Mary said without even looking up to see what Annie was calling her out for.

"I *know* you've been snooping, and this is *proof*!" Annie said.

Of course, she did not know this at all, and Lord Tennyson had to endure their bickering for an entire twelve hours until Ezra *finally* burst out, "Take it to the Sibling Council because I'm sick of you both!"

Lord Tennyson's plan had worked!

The next morning, before the McNiff children were due to put on their church clothes, they climbed the ladder to the treehouse in the backyard. With Ezra's help, Lord Tennyson, who had Sweetums hanging around his neck and middle, was hoisted up and inside. The treehouse was always the location of the Sibling Council, but it was more of a platform with a few planks for walls, a highly unsafe destination for children and respectable dogs. He looked down and felt woozy from the height.

He kept Sweetums tucked safely next to him as they all sat together in a circle.

As the oldest, Annie began as always. "I call this meeting to order!"

Lord Tennyson nudged Ezra, a more neutral sibling, to speak up before the fight could break out afresh. Looking nervous, Ezra cleared his throat.

"Uh, the both of you need to stop being annoying."

This was not how Lord Tennyson would have begun.

Annie ignored this and held up a piece of paper she'd pulled from the printer that morning.

"As Queen of the Sibling Council, I have a document Mary is required to sign if she wants to remain a member."

"What document?" Mary demanded. "Who wrote it? Are you all against me?"

"I didn't write it," Ezra protested. Pearl and Tate shook their heads too.

"I wrote it on behalf of all of us," Annie said. "It's for your own good, and for the good of everyone in the circle."

Mary looked at Lord Tennyson. He quickly nudged her knee to let her know he didn't take sides.

"Well, read it, then," Ezra said.

Annie cleared her throat and began to read.

I, Mary McNiff, do confess to petty theft and trespassing on multiple occasions.

I do confess to stealing the following items, as well as multiple others. These items include:

-The key to Annie's safe

-Annie's earrings*

-Ezra's Christmas chocolate

-A bar of soap from the teacher's bathroom

-Other things we know she took but can't remember

*indicates multiple offenses

Further, I confess to invasion of privacy on multiple occasions.

I have gone through all my siblings' belongings more than once.

I swear not to commit such acts of larceny or trespassing ever again,** and to pay $1.00 in damages to Ezra and Annie. Signed

_____

(Mary McNiff)

**If I do, I will submit to penance as determined by the Sibling Council or be kicked out completely.

The children erupted into laughter, including Mary.

"It's *not* a joke," Annie said. "It's all true, and Mary must sign—in red marker to symbolize a blood oath."

"Or what?" Mary said.

Annie's voice became low and scathing. "You know what happened to Anne Boleyn, don't you?"

Mary rolled her eyes.

"What happened?" Tate and Pearl cried.

"Off with her head!" Annie yelled.

Tate and Pearl screamed.

Lord Tennyson shook his head. Mr. McNiff's dramatic gene was very strong indeed.

"I don't have a red marker," Mary said breezily. "Unless you really want me to sign with blood." She pretended to bite her finger for effect.

Tate and Pearl gasped.

Lord Tennyson raised his head and Mary stopped.

"We have to take a vote," Mary said. "All in favor of kicking me out of the Sibling Council, which isn't even legal because I'm a *sibling*." Only Annie raised her hand.

"You lose," Mary said.

"Not yet. Ezra, you called this meeting because you know what a rat Mary is," Annie said. "You choose how she should be punished."

"Uh . . ."

Mary raised a sharp eyebrow, cowing him.

Lord Tennyson could see Ezra had something to say and wished he would, but Annie and Mary began to argue fiercely.

"I didn't *steal* your key or your stupid diary," Mary said, stretching the truth. "It's in your safe, isn't it? Also, Ezra's chocolate was so old it was practically moldy—someone had to eat it!"

"That's beside the point," Annie said. "Isn't it, Ezra?"

Ezra opened his mouth, but nothing came out.

"No," Mary said. "It's not." Then she smiled, stood, and jumped down from the treehouse, swinging on a tree branch to break her fall before hitting the ground in a most spectacular somersault.

Ezra got that look in his eye that said he had to follow in similar fashion.

"I haven't adjourned our meeting!" Annie yelled after her. "Admit your guilt!"

"I don't have to admit anything!" Mary said. "Dad is calling. Time for church, you wicked sister!"

Ezra jumped, mimicking Mary's acrobatics, while the rest climbed down from the treehouse and ran after Annie, who was chasing Mary, leaving Lord Tennyson alone, unable to get down on his own. They had at least remembered Sweetums, who was carried over Ezra's shoulder, squawking, her arms outstretched to Lord Tennyson as he was left behind. He pondered how well the meeting had gone. Perhaps not well at all. No peace had been made, and neither Annie nor Mary was backing down. Oh dear. He settled into a nap, knowing he would likely be waiting a long time for the children to remember where he was. While he wasn't in the pews at church with the McNiffs, he sincerely hoped they were learning to repent!

CHAPTER EIGHT

Pedaling the Family Bike

AS PREDICTED, IT HAD TAKEN THE CHILDREN SEVERAL hours after church to remember that the last place they had seen Lord Tennyson was in the treehouse. Seeing their worried, tearstained faces united at the bottom of the ladder gave him a sliver of hope for their future as compassionate human beings. He was still enjoying the children's new-found gratitude for his delightful company the next morning when Annie and Mary kissed him good-bye before riding their bikes into town to meet friends, their tempers somewhat settled.

As Tate and Pearl watched them leave, Honey tilted her head and said, "Two children named Tate and Pearl need to learn to ride bikes like their sisters. Go on, Lord Tennyson will watch you. And meanwhile, I'll feed Osbert!" She wrinkled her eyes at the sourdough pet that had continued to grow into what looked like an actual monster blob. Lord Tennyson was slightly afraid of it, and now the monster had a name! Lord Tennyson slowly backed away, wondering when it would start talking, and if Osbert would be one more creature he would have to mind.

Sweetums popped her pacifier into her mouth and climbed aboard Lord Tennyson. They passed the chicks, whom he could hear flapping their new feathers. He paused to deeply inhale, gulping at the memory of past birds, before leading Pearl and Tate outside.

"I don't know how to ride," Pearl said. "I'll fall off."

"We'll ride together!" Tate said, pushing up his red glasses, looking eagerly for the bikes.

Lord Tennyson furrowed his furry brow, wondering how to separate them. Learning to ride a bike on the same bike would only make things more difficult and make Pearl more reliant on Tate. This morning he would teach them how much fun riding a bike all by themselves was. He himself had only ridden a handful of times in Honey's bike basket, and it was one of his great sorrows that the McNiffs had never thought of buying him a bike of his own.

Using his paw, Lord Tennyson lifted the garage door an inch, prompting Pearl and Tate to push it up farther. There they sat: the faithful old beginner bikes, hand-me-downs from their older sisters and brother, who had gotten them used from neighbors and friends.

Tate looked longingly at Ezra, who was riding in circles on the driveway on his *new* bike, the one he had saved up to buy with his own money.

Lord Tennyson pulled the helmets from the bottom shelves and coaxed the children to wheel two of the bikes onto the grass, all while Sweetums pulled on his beard and attempted to store her pacifier in his right ear. He responded by gently tipping her off into the grass just as the two bunnies, now officially named Felicity and Delilah, came hopping out the front door. He shook the pacifier out of his ear, and it landed in the dirt. With Sweetums busy chasing bunnies, she didn't notice. Thankfully, that meant Lord Tennyson could focus on bike riding. However, he quickly realized, as he had never had a bike of his own, he didn't know how to teach it.

He recruited Ezra by pulling on his sock with his teeth.

"All right, all right," Ezra said, following him to the grass.

"I can't! I can't! I can't!" Pearl cried. "I'll fall off."

Lord Tennyson looked at Tate.

"I could try firtht," Tate suggested.

Nodding, Lord Tennyson nudged Tate's feet up to the pedals. Under his supervision, Ezra pushed the back of Tate's bike while they both ran on either side of Tate, nudging him upright if he threatened to tip over.

"Thee, Pearl!" Tate shouted. "It'th eathy!"

But Pearl sat on her bike, shaking her head.

Lord Tennyson knew Pearl could be brave; after all, hadn't she saved the bunnies from becoming rabbit stew? She just had to try! He pulled on her sock, then nudged her tires. He even chased Felicity and Delilah out from under a bush, where they were hiding from Sweetums, hoping this would make her laugh and forget her fears. Finally, Pearl bit her lip, closed her eyes, and pedaled hard. She was off! Ezra and Lord Tennyson ran alongside her as she sailed all the way across the yard.

You see, Pearl, he barked happily, *when you step into bravery, the world bends to your will!*

Her previous wailing turned to a look of wonder.

Ezra, Tate, and Sweetums cheered.

"See?" Ezra said. "You learned together, but you both did it on your own!"

Tate's face shone with a newfound pride.

When Lord Tennyson ran away from the bunnies, who were now chasing *him*, he caught a glimpse of Mr. McNiff standing in the driveway watching, his eyes a bit misty.

"Now, children." Mr. McNiff's voice echoed from underneath the medieval knight mask on his face as he paced back and forth in the living room later that evening. An emergency McNiff Family Council had been called that night after dinner. Though Mr. McNiff had called the meeting, he was also in the middle of trying on his lead actor's Don Quixote costume, hence the mask. Lord

Tennyson sat at Honey's feet, admiring Mr. McNiff's glorious getup.

"It has once again come to my attention that there are six children residing in this home all day long."

"Whoa!" Tate shouted. "That'th a lot of kidth."

"Indeed," Mr. McNiff said. "Six *slovenly* children." He paused and looked at the children behind his mask. They shrank back where they sat crammed together on the couch.

"*Dad,*" Annie said. "It's summer vacation."

"That's why we're all home!" Pearl exclaimed.

"Aha!" Mr. McNiff said. "I knew there was a reason."

He paced, his armor clanging. The children giggled.

"But we still must remember the discussion we had about summer," Honey reminded them.

"Once again," Mr. McNiff said, "we are backsliding."

Mr. McNiff tried to pick up a filthy sock from the living room rug but couldn't bend down far enough in his armor. "Dirty laundry in the living room."

Lord Tennyson eyed the children as they assigned one another blame.

"That's not mine!"

"It's Ezra's!"

"No it's not!"

"Silence!" Mr. McNiff said, his voice echoing in the armor.

The children fell silent.

"Here is your new summer chore chart," Honey said, holding up a large poster board.

Lord Tennyson wished he had thought to make a summer chore chart. It was so beautifully done in Honey's handwriting and color coded by buddies. Oh, he reveled in such organization!

As usual, Annie was matched with Sweetums.

Ezra was matched with Tate.

And Mary was with Pearl.

"Sweetums can't even do any work!" Annie said. "It's not fair."

"Fair!" Sweetums yelled, pulling fistfuls of Lord Tennyson's hair.

"But Mary's about to leave for camp," said Pearl.

"Together," Mr. McNiff interrupted, "we can keep this home as clean as a whistle!"

"How clean ith a whithle?" Tate asked, confused.

"Well, at the very least we shouldn't live like Mr. Goody's barnyard animals," Mr. McNiff said. "Which brings me to my next point: this house is turning into a zoo!"

"I love the thoo!" Tate said. "Ethpethially the thn . . ." Ezra gave him a hard look to be quiet.

"Nine pets! Two rabbits hopping around the house, six chicks atop the kitchen table, and, of course, Lord Tennyson."

Lord Tennyson looked up, surprised. He was always taken aback to hear himself described as a "pet." He was obviously no mere pet, though he supposed that was how he would look to outsiders.

He felt Ezra exhale. His precious snake was still a secret, safely coiled up in a shoebox in his bedroom.

"Speaking of Lord Tennyson," Mr. McNiff continued, but a wrestling match had ensued, and it took the knight in armor, Honey, and Lord Tennyson to reassemble the six children quietly back onto the couch.

Mr. McNiff cleared his throat. "As I was saying, this morning I witnessed something quite inspirational. Did you know that right here in our midst . . . is a brilliant schnauzer?"

Lord Tennyson sat up.

"Lord Tennyson taught Pearl and Tate how to ride a bike. He also taught *me* something."

Lord Tennyson straightened further, tall and proud.

"I helped," Ezra interjected.

"Yes, exactly my point! Lord Tennyson showed me that our whole family is actually pedaling the *same* bike," Mr. McNiff said.

The children groaned, but Lord Tennyson nodded, prodding him on. He loved Mr. McNiff's parenting analogies.

"Now, now," Mr. McNiff said. "This is a good one. As a family, we all sit atop the same bike, do we not? And if we all pedal, the bike moves forward. But if any one person stops pedaling or drags their feet on the ground, it makes pedaling harder for everyone else—and sometimes even causes the bike to fall over." He stopped and looked at each of the children.

"I like biketh," Tate said. "I'm going to get a new bike for my nektht birthday tho I can ride like Ethra."

"What if our bike is broken?" Ezra asked.

"I have a flat tire," Mary said crossly. "Annie did it."

"That doesn't even make sense!" Annie said.

"Children, this is exactly what your father is talking about," Honey interrupted. "Pedaling the family bike is merely an analogy for a happier family life. All of us must think about pedaling *with* the family instead of against it."

The children looked skeptical, but Lord Tennyson beamed.

"And so, because he inspired it, Lord Tennyson can oversee your new chore assignments," Honey said.

His hard work had paid off! There would be no "real nanny" or "more help" talk now, surely. He would see to it that they started right away. An early bedtime would help. If only he had a whistle that he could blow, like Mary Poppins. He would blow the whistle and all the children would march obediently upstairs for a bath, a story, and soothing lullabies.

Instead, the children pig-piled on top of one another, laughing until Pearl and Tate cried from getting squished and Mary burped in Annie's face and Ezra jumped on the furniture.

Mr. McNiff and Honey exchanged a knowing, weary look that concerned Lord Tennyson again, even after the brilliant schnauzer comment.

He began practicing his own whistle in earnest, but this backfired since Sweetums thought he was spitting. And, well, she loved to mimic. He buried his head in the pink pouf on the couch to stay dry, trying to think of a way to accomplish these new responsibilities.

CHAPTER NINE

A Sister's Revenge

ANOTHER WEEK PASSED. ANNIE AND MARY WERE NOT pedaling the same bike as Mr. McNiff had asked. The day before swim camp, Honey sent Mary up to pack while the rest of the family played badminton, another sport Mr. McNiff did not excel at. After Lord Tennyson had convinced Pearl to at least hold the racket, he went upstairs with Mary.

Instead of finding shorts and shirts for camp, though, she skipped over to Annie's new hiding place (her sock drawer), found the key, and once again opened the safe.

Mary's treachery was becoming quite a bad habit; she just couldn't seem to stop reading the diary. Both Lord Tennyson and Mary were learning a lot about Annie, though. For instance, Annie didn't like school lunch on Thursdays and Fridays. She loved the hand-me-downs she got from their neighbor Christie Lundeen but was embarrassed when Megan asked where she'd gotten them.

Mostly Annie wrote about things like school and friends and lunch, but Mary's favorite entries of course were about her sister's great love for Cal Hubbard. Lord Tennyson stared. After the failure at the Sibling Council, he had not yet figured out a better way to stop this invasion of privacy.

Not liking the disapproving look on his face, Mary reached for Lord Tennyson.

"Oh, Tenny boy, you're such a good boy," she crooned, scratching his ears just how he liked until she . . . placed him in her closet and shut the door.

He protested loudly at her trickery, whining and scratching the inside of the door. How rude. He did not like the dark, hot closet, especially during the summer.

"I'll let you out," Mary said from the other side of the closet door, "if you promise to be quiet and not tattle." She opened the door a crack. He frowned at her. He would *not* be bribed.

Mary relented anyway, kneeling and opening the door. "I love you, and I'm sorry for putting you in the closet. Please forgive me." Perhaps he would if she handed over the diary. He gently tried to pry the diary out of her hands without leaving more bite marks, but he only succeeded in ripping a page out. Oh no!

They both gaped at the wet, torn paper in front of them. Mary began to read.

Dear Diary,

I've had it! I wish I were an only child. My brothers and sisters are so annoying I can't stand them! Especially Mary. Why do I have to share a room with such a slob? She's almost twelve years old and she still wets the bed! I . . .

Mary grabbed the paper and crumpled it angrily into a ball.

Lord Tennyson shook out his fur and lay down. He thought about comforting Mary after hearing those mean words or helping her to hide the evidence again, but no,

112

he had warned her and she refused to listen. It was time to face the consequences of her actions, whatever they may be.

Mary pulled at the little bits of paper stuck in the margin of the diary, trying to make it look like there hadn't been a page there at all.

"Don't say anything," Mary said, trying to smooth out the piece of paper. "I know I shouldn't have read it, but . . . Don't look at me like that!"

Lord Tennyson cocked his head and sternly communicated, *Oh yes, I will look at you like that.*

"Tenny, stop it!" she said crossly. "How would you like it if your sister hated you and wrote about you in a diary? I don't even wet the bed anymore. She even tried to get me kicked out of the Sibling Council! You're lucky that dogs can't read or write!"

Lord Tennyson raised an eyebrow. Actually, he had learned quite a bit from teaching all the McNiff children to read. He had nudged their hands as they practiced their letters so many times that he was likely the most literate member of the family! Although he would be very content to never read *Fluffy Snuffie Schnauzer Learns to Bark* ever again.

After replacing the key and diary, Mary carefully ripped the torn paper into a hundred tiny pieces before burying them at the very bottom of the small trash can.

Brooding, Mary pulled out shorts and shirts from random drawers. Even though Lord Tennyson had taught her how to sort, nothing was organized because she was always so impatient to put laundry away. None of her socks matched, and all had holes in them. Mary opened Annie's drawers and, without asking, borrowed two pairs.

"You'll miss me, won't you? Even if she doesn't?" Mary said.

Of course he would, no matter how naughty she might be. Lord Tennyson put his nose to her legs to make sure she knew.

"Mrs. Annie McNiff Hubbard," Mary said out loud. "That's what her diary says, Tenny. She probably wants to run away with him so she can get away from me."

Mary paused midpacking like she'd been struck by the world's largest lightning bolt. There was *that* look on her face—the look she'd had when she put a tadpole in Annie's soup last summer.

Lord Tennyson made a low growl.

"You should try smiling," Mary said to him. "Smiling makes people happier. That's what Daddy always says." She tried to pull his mouth up. "There! Isn't that better?"

Lord Tennyson wiggled away from her reach and readjusted his lips.

She bent over at the waist, laughing. "Oh, Tenny, it's my best idea ever—you'll think it's screamingly funny."

He highly doubted that.

That night, after he had tucked the little ones into bed, Lord Tennyson slept on the floor of Mary and Annie's room. Despite his efforts to build upon the bike analogy, he couldn't get Tate to sleep in his own bed in Ezra's room because Tate said he wouldn't hear Pearl if she called for him. Lord Tennyson would have to think about this later. Tonight, he was focused on the foreboding he felt, like an incoming storm. At bedtime, Mary had been suspiciously solicitous (meaning especially sweet) to Annie.

Something was *definitely* amiss.

When Annie had said good night to Mary and told her to have fun at camp, Lord Tennyson had hoped Mary would have a change of heart about whatever she was plotting to do next.

But long after Annie was asleep, Lord Tennyson could sense Mary staring at the clock—and it had nothing to do with the wet-alarm. He longed for rest, and the minutes felt like hours ticking more slowly than Sweetums learning to walk. Lord Tennyson dozed a couple of times but couldn't allow himself to fall into a deep sleep, not with Mary awake. *Tick, tick, tick, tick.* Mary tossed from one side to the other. Lord Tennyson tossed from one position to the next.

He tried to *will* her to fall asleep, and it almost worked. Sometime around 10:45 p.m. she dozed, but then she quickly sat up, remaining in a frozen position until 10:55. Confident that Annie had not woken, Mary slowly swung her legs over the bed and stepped over him. He stumbled after her down the hallway, his nails clicking on the floor as Mary crept carefully to avoid the squeaky places. Hearing the clicking, she looked back at him.

"Shush, Tenny! Go back to bed."

He would do no such thing!

When Mary turned back around, she bumped right into Honey and gasped.

"Goodness!" Honey said sleepily. "You're walking down the hall like a cartoon character."

"I'm . . . I'm . . . ," Mary said, then hugged her mother around the waist while she stalled for an excuse.

Her mother laughed softly. "Sweet girl. Are you too excited to sleep?"

Mary froze, eyes wide, wondering what she was supposed to be excited for.

"Get to bed, and I'll see you in the morning for your big camp adventure."

"Camp!" Mary said. "Yes, that!"

Lord Tennyson followed Mary into the bathroom, but she was not deterred.

"Go to sleep," she said crossly. "You're going to get me in trouble!"

Lord Tennyson did not go to sleep. He would have liked to point out that it was Mary who was going to get *herself* in trouble.

After a few moments Mary peeked back out of the bathroom.

Honey's door was partially closed now, but Mr. McNiff was still up. They could hear one of his favorite musicals,

Seven Brides for Seven Brothers, playing downstairs on the TV. Mr. McNiff was always watching old musicals to get ideas for his theater productions.

"Ezra!" Mary whispered, jumping onto his bed. "Ezra!"

"No," he said drowsily. "She'll murder you."

"Ezra, come on. You said you would."

Lord Tennyson was surprised. A secret plan had been hatched and he didn't know about it?

"Tired."

"Come on, don't be a chicken!"

Lord Tennyson's ears perked up. Chickens? The chicks were downstairs unattended, and suddenly he could smell them.

"Ezra, please?"

No answer.

"Ezzie, I'm leaving right now with or without you!"

Mary waited expectantly for him to sit up. And he did, as he always did, his eyes shining as if under the spell of Mary and one of her so-called adventures.

Lord Tennyson shook his head.

"Mary . . . ," Ezra began.

"We won't get caught!"

"Remember the phone call where you pretended to—"

"Ezra, that was a good one!"

"And toilet papering the band teacher's—"

"You *know* that was fun!"

The negotiation went on until finally Ezra was bribed with a dollar and five favors, the McNiffs' favorite form of currency, redeemable after Mary came home from camp. Lord Tennyson put his paws on Ezra's bed, hoping he could trap him under the covers, but he was no longer a match for his boy.

Ezra pulled back the covers, and together he and Mary crept down the stairs, followed by the tap-tap of Lord Tennyson's toenails on the wooden stairs.

Mary climbed up onto the kitchen sink. Very slowly, she opened the kitchen window.

Lord Tennyson growled a warning, just low enough for them to hear.

"Tenny, please," Mary said. "Ez, get him a dog treat."

A dog treat! As if a mere dog treat would pacify him. Who did they think was in charge here?

But Ezra fetched him one: his favorite, a small chicken-liver cracker, and it *was* delicious.

Lord Tennyson was conflicted. He wanted to be loyal to both the children *and* the parents. Barking would stop the mischief before it started, but it would also possibly suggest he really wasn't up to the task of caretaking. Additionally, he would undoubtedly wake Sweetums, and for the next two hours she would be rolling around making messes and endangering her life in the dark, *and* she would end up being a crab apple the next day. Still, he could not let his children leave this house while his dear mister slept peacefully in a recliner. There was only one solution: he would have to go with them.

Mary stuck one leg out the window.

"The back door is open," Ezra whispered.

"You don't sneak out of the house through a door!"

Lord Tennyson swallowed his cracker. He looked at Mary and back into the living room, letting out a last-ditch-effort whine, hoping she'd reconsider.

It hadn't been loud, but Ezra lunged for him all the same, and Mary froze halfway through the window. Ezra held Lord Tennyson's mouth shut tightly as all three of them stayed as still as statues.

A loud snore echoed through the room.

"We have to bring him," Ezra said, his hand still clamping Lord Tennyson's jaw shut in a very undignified manner.

"No!" Mary said, while Lord Tennyson nodded a vigorous yes.

Without asking Mary's permission again, Ezra picked him up and walked right out the back door while Mary scrambled through the kitchen window.

The bike ride into town was dark and spooky in the moonlight. Lord Tennyson would have liked to ride in Mary's basket but it was suspiciously full, so he chased after them on his bad knees. What other choice did he have?

"I'm glad Tenny's with us after all," Mary whispered. "Look at the moon. It's a night for ghosts and goblins."

Lord Tennyson shivered as his heart raced.

It was only a mile into town, but a mile in the dark was far different from a mile during the day. Bats swooped silently above their heads, and the strong smell of water buffalo wafted through the air. When they passed old Mrs. Gage's house, Lord Tennyson growled as he pictured Fat Cat curled on the end of Mrs. Gage's bed, not having to worry about or chase after misbehaving children. And then, as if the night couldn't get any more ominous, there came a terrifying sound—the long, lonely howl of the coyotes deep in the forest. Lord Tennyson had never actually seen them, but every once in a while he could hear and sense their presence, lurking closer than his people ever knew.

He ran faster, then faster still, until every muscle in his body became too tired to sprint and he had to slow, heavily panting. The children got farther ahead. Lord Tennyson was reminded that he wasn't as young as he used to be, and he certainly wasn't accustomed to sneaking out of the house and running after two juvenile delinquents. A small creeping doubt in his ability to properly mind his children nagged at him. No, he just needed more rest and fewer midnight adventures.

He turned onto Main Street, where the shops were silent and dark, bathed only by the light of the moon and the occasional street bulb. Lord Tennyson continued on until catching up to Mary and Ezra in front of the old library fence that was desperately in need of a new paint job.

Mary was holding a can of spray paint, but it wasn't to

spruce the fence up. She was painting words on it in bright pink!

Winded and barely able to move, Lord Tennyson stared, shocked.

True Love by Old Mother Hubbard. When I'm lonely or feeling sad . . . he read. Oh dear. This was worse than he'd even imagined.

"Mary, that's enough!" Ezra whispered.

Mary laughed. "Keep reading, Ezzie!"

Lord Tennyson staggered over to reason with her, but to no avail. Ezra read and Mary sprayed right over Lord Tennyson, making large loopy pink letters on the fence. He grabbed hold of the hem of her pajama pants.

"Stop it," she said. "Or I'll spray *you* pink!"

Lord Tennyson didn't doubt this was true. He could already feel where a few droplets of pink spray paint had landed atop his head.

"It's a very bad poem," she whispered. "Maybe the worst ever—and that's why it's so good!" Mary cackled and sprayed, undeterred.

Unable to stop her, Lord Tennyson moved silently out of the way and lay down on his exhausted paws, defeated.

CHAPTER TEN

A Tea Party with Lord Tennyson

"I LOVE HAVING A CLEAN ROOM WITHOUT THE BEAST
here," Annie said right after Mary left for swim camp the
next morning.

Lord Tennyson's heart thumped uneasily in his chest as
he swiped absently at his head.

Mary and Ezra had wiped the top of Lord Tennyson's
head with a baby wipe, and he had rolled around in the
grass, but the hair on top of his head still had a smattering

of tiny pink droplets no one seemed to know the source of.

Amid his inner turmoil, Annie hummed and continued to organize her pencils in order of the rainbow. He paced and reread the note Mary had left on Annie's mirror.

Dear Annie,

I'll miss you! I hope you'll miss me when you're all alone at night in the dark by yourself. I'll think of you every day if I'm not having too much fun—please write and tell me how the chicks are doing! Don't let Tenny eat them!

Your favorite sister, Mary

P.S. Make sure to come pick me up at the library on Saturday—don't let Mom and Dad forget!

LIBRARY on Saturday. Saturday. Saturday.

Make sure to come get me.

"Poor Mary!" Annie laughed. "She thinks we might forget to pick her up!"

Actually, this was always a possibility with Honey and Mr. McNiff. Lord Tennyson had a hopeful thought. Maybe they *would* forget to pick her up and Lord Tennyson would

126

fetch her himself. Maybe he could coax her into repainting the fence before Annie even saw it. If that didn't work, he could stage a sickness and throw up on the living room rug so Annie would stay home with him!

He thought more on this as Annie thoroughly cleaned her shared room like a happy Cinderella, emptying all the drawers and folding all the clothes (even Mary's!). She organized their desk and purged it of every unsightly crumb and scrap of paper. She even dusted the windowsills and washed the windowpanes while Lord Tennyson pulled the trash bags down to the kitchen. Unfortunately, the bags had split open and Mr. McNiff had tsked him, thinking he was trying to eat the contents. In part, it was true. The teeny-tiny pieces that Mary had ripped out and buried in the trash had fluttered out. To keep the peace, Lord Tennyson had lapped them all up, and his stomach was now full of paper.

Lord Tennyson could see Annie's point of view. Without Mary's hurricane habits, the room stayed clean, with clothes, books, and paper all in their proper places. Lord Tennyson felt more settled when walking in. He hoped that when Mary returned, she would see that cleanliness really was good for her soul . . . and for her relationship with Annie.

But oh, it was quiet.

Lord Tennyson was pleased to see that after just three days without her sister, even Annie thought it was a little *too* quiet.

"I'm actually starting to miss her," Annie whispered in his ear that night. "How weird."

He may have been able to feel all-the-way happy about this excellent development except for that *one little thing* Mary had done to the library fence the night before leaving for camp.

Lord Tennyson was happily distracted, though, by a tea party, orchestrated by Tate after Pearl had been too nervous to attend a preschool friend's birthday party without Tate.

With Sweetums safely napping upstairs, Pearl, Nicholas, and Tate sat in the small porch that doubled as a playroom and greenhouse, just off the kitchen. It was a room made of tall windows and full of warm sunlight, though today it was rainy and overcast. In theory, it was an ideal room where Honey could see them while she dug potatoes or plucked pea pods in the backyard. But it was

Lord Tennyson, of course, who kept the best watch.

The tea party was also a reward for another successful bike riding lesson Lord Tennyson had given Pearl and Tate, who had gotten all the way down the road without help from Ezra. Meanwhile, Honey had used part of the sourdough monster, Osbert, to bake a loaf of bread. Osbert had not made a sound when half of it was put into the oven—it only continued to grow! Lord Tennyson did not know what to make of this creature, but he kept a warning eye on it when the children were in close vicinity.

The younger McNiffs were not allowed to drink real tea or hot chocolate from their teapots, as Mr. McNiff had banned any liquid other than water outside the kitchen after one particularly giant chocolate-milk puddle had traveled from the playroom to the living room to the now-stained cream carpet in the bedrooms upstairs. So Pearl, Nicholas, and Tate had to be content with mere water.

No matter, the McNiffs had great imaginations and could pretend the water was anything at all, even pinkalicious cotton candy (Tate's favorite) or peppermint ice cream topped with whipped cream, sprinkles, and a chocolate Easter rabbit (Pearl's favorite).

Pearl was *very* excited for the tea party this afternoon because she had a new idea.

"I'm going to make a new flavor, Nicholas boy," she said. Lord Tennyson could see that this new flavor was not purely imaginary but composed of freshly picked dandelions and a large pile of rocks. He grimaced inwardly while nodding his head at Pearl, encouraging her to take the initiative.

"Nicholas is very excited," she whispered to Lord Tennyson, who sniffed Nicholas and his perpetually plastic smell. Nicholas was a very curious fellow; he looked so real, but his facial muscles never changed, and his hair was always perfectly placed. The only blemish on Nicholas was the teeth marks on either side of his perfectly combed hair, from Sweetums, of course. Even then, Nicholas had not changed expressions. Pearl spoke to him as if he spoke back. And even with his superior hearing, Lord Tennyson had never heard Nicholas make a sound.

But as Pearl gathered up her ingredients, her look of excitement morphed into a frown. She turned to Tate.

"Our teapot is missing."

What she didn't know was that Ezra had been using it

as a grasshopper sanctuary before Annie confiscated it for a display of wildflowers, imagining what it would be like if Cal gave her such a bouquet. Hoping to avoid a kerfuffle with their older sister, Lord Tennyson hoped Pearl and Tate would simply find an alternative.

"How about . . . ?" Tate looked very thoughtful as he raised his chin high up in the air. His eyes came to rest on a small square box on the highest shelf in the playroom. "That one."

"Tatey, we can't," Pearl whispered to Tate, her eyes growing wide.

"It'th our only hope," Tate whispered back.

"It's Annie's special Winnie-the-Pooh pot. It's *glass*."

"We should get it down," Tate whispered back, undeterred.

"Annie would be very, very, *very* mad."

"Tenny will protect uth," Tate said, grabbing Lord Tennyson around his neck and affectionately sitting on him.

Pearl looked from Lord Tennyson to Nicholas. Lord Tennyson frowned at Nicholas, who was still smiling, giving the go-ahead, when the idea was clearly a very bad one.

Their pet bunnies, Felicity and Delilah, hopped around the room, giving no advice but pausing to sniff Lord Tennyson. He stood very still, unwilling to admit that he was still scared of the bunnies and their claws and teeth.

Pearl, Tate, and Lord Tennyson looked up at the precious box that held Annie's prized teapot.

"Look at those adorable cups!" Pearl said, enraptured.

"We can't rethitht," Tate said, as if this settled it.

Accompanying the teapot were indeed four adorable and tiny china teacups that Pearl had always wanted to sip from. On each cup was a painting of Owl, Tigger, Rabbit, Eeyore, and Baby Roo. Realizing Pearl was serious about this endeavor, Lord Tennyson ignored the bunnies and shook out his fur.

"We'll put it right back," Tate said. "Thacred honor."

Lord Tennyson looked away as a sign of dissent.

Pearl looked up. "I can't reach it."

Tate pushed a small plastic chair over for her to stand on.

"I still can't reach," Pearl said after climbing up. "Hmm. I know." She pulled the small children's table over to the bookshelf and hefted the small chair atop it. Pearl and Tate looked at Lord Tennyson hopefully, wanting him to say yes.

"Oh, Tenny, be a good boy," Pearl said. Lord Tennyson wondered what this really meant, to be a "good boy." If he were really a good boy, he would tattle on Pearl and Tate by barking, which would alert Honey in the garden.

Then again, Pearl was not especially brave and daring like Mary. She was not bold and assertive like Annie nor ruthless like Sweetums, nor confident like Tate, nor strong like Ezra! Little Pearl was timid, but here she was trying to be a bit brave all on her own.

And so, Lord Tennyson put one paw on the precariously perched chair atop the table, to support the climb under his supervision. Like her courage, the chair wobbled.

But Pearl gave him her bravest smile.

"Thithy!" Tate whispered. "You got it!"

Pearl stood on her tiptoes and reached up. Only the very tips of her fingers could touch the box.

Realizing she still wasn't tall enough, Pearl made the mistake of looking down. She was suddenly clinging to the bookshelf, frozen with fear.

"You got it," Tate said. "Jutht grab it."

"It's too high," Pearl said. "I'm scared. Save me."

Lord Tennyson knew she *needed* to do this. She *needed*

to reach. He looked up at her and told her with his eyes that she *could* reach the box.

Pearl whimpered louder.

"Jump and hit the box and I will catch it," Tate suggested.

Lord Tennyson thought this sounded like a good plan except for the part about her jumping and the part about the box falling and hoping Tate could catch it.

The chair creaked. Pearl froze again.

"What if the chair breaks? What if I fall?"

"Then we'll get to go to the emergenthy room!" Tate said, a little too excitedly.

Pearl peeked at Lord Tennyson again. He held her gaze.

The chair wobbled back and forth.

"Get it!" Tate and Lord Tennyson shouted at the same time (in their own way).

Pearl hopped lightly and hit the box from underneath. It moved an inch toward her. She hopped again and then one more time until it came toppling toward her . . . at the same time as the chair toppled. Tate screamed and held out his arms. Lord Tennyson reacted as quickly as possible,

shifting a pile of dress-up clothes so that the three of them ended up on a big cushioned heap on the floor.

"Thithy," Tate said admiringly, adjusting his glasses. "You did it!"

Lord Tennyson checked for broken bones and blood and, finding none, let Pearl scramble to the teapot box. It was miraculously intact, sitting on the floor. Exultant, Pearl patted Lord Tennyson on the head. He exhaled deeply.

"He'th a thuper dog," Tate said. "Better than Thuperman, Batman, and Thpider-Man combined."

Pearl and Tate pulled a long pink dress-up costume over the table for a tablecloth and set out the four china Pooh cups with the matching saucers. They looked in reverence at the tiny cups, with nary a chip or a scratch on any of them—highly unusual for anything the McNiffs owned.

"So pretty," Pearl said.

"Let'th fill up the teapot," Tate whispered.

"Stay right here," Pearl said, wagging her finger at Nicholas. "Don't move a muscle." Which of course he didn't.

Pearl and Tate liked to use the outside hose normally, but today they went into the kitchen and pulled a chair to the kitchen sink to fill the precious teapot. Lord Tennyson kept an eye on Osbert, while also hoping the children would use the small sugar cubes he liked to chomp on.

The teapot filled and carefully carried back, Lord Tennyson climbed onto one of the four chairs, facing Nicholas, who sat on the table. Pearl stirred the dandelions with a stick and dropped in a few more favorite rocks for extra flavor. Lord Tennyson used his tongue to drink his "tea" while Nicholas did nothing except smile his immovable smile.

"Here, kitty, kitty, kitties," Pearl called.

Lord Tennyson turned his head to see Widdy Boo and Nuff saunter by outside the windows. But he growled when Fat Cat herself appeared. Pearl, a lover of all furry friends, quickly opened the door and wrangled all the wet cats under both her arms. But it was Fat Cat whom she chose to set on a chair across from Lord Tennyson. He stayed still and stoic only because it was important to show the children to be polite in the company of one's adversary. Lord Tennyson's whiskers twitched in mirth at the look on Fat Cat's face when Pearl then found a bonnet and a doll dress for Fat Cat to wear. She was compliant of course because

Pearl shared cookie pieces and let her take little licks out of the china teacups.

Never would he have guessed that he would be at the same table as his great antagonist. All went surprisingly well until an upstairs door opened and footsteps came down the stairs. Lord Tennyson's ears pointed upward in full alert—Annie was coming! As if floating on air, Annie twirled past the playroom with a smile on her face, humming. Pearl and Tate glanced from the tea set to each other in terror until suddenly Annie stopped and stared at them.

"Fat Cat!" she exclaimed, opening the door to the screened porch. "What adorable clothes!" Widdy Boo and Nuff appeared from underneath the table and cozied around Annie's legs. Annie smiled, knelt at the table, and lifted the teapot to pour some tea. It was then that she froze.

Pearl, Tate, and Lord Tennyson smiled weakly.

Fat Cat, sensing the mood shift, jumped from her chair and sauntered outside with the cousin entourage, still dressed in a bonnet and doll dress. Annie began to huff and puff like the Big Bad Wolf about to blow down little pig houses, but Pearl and Tate were saved from death because just at that moment Honey walked through the door, her arms full of vegetables.

Her face softened as only a parent's can when children are playing well together.

"A tea party! Oh, Tenny, aren't you the most wonderful. And, Annie! How kind to let them use your special tea set." Honey blew them a kiss before continuing on to the kitchen.

They peeked up at Annie.

"You should have asked before using *my very special tea set*," she finally said.

"But you alwayth thay no," Tate burst out.

"And I couldn't find mine," Pearl said, looking at Annie with her big eyes. Lord Tennyson nudged Annie, reminding her *why* Pearl couldn't find it.

Annie nodded, remembering. "I'm sorry. I used it, and I should have asked too. Now, Lady Pearl, please pass the sugar."

"It's not real thugar," Tate said. "We are pretending."

"Of course you are," Annie said. "It's called imagination, of which I have plenty. Please pass the sugar, royal subject, and have some manners. The queen is in your presence."

Lord Tennyson resumed his position at the table.

Pearl poured the pretend tea and Tate passed the pretend sugar.

"Anything else, your majesty?" Pearl bowed.

"Yes," Annie said. "A toast." They clinked the small teacups and Annie said, "To me, the queen—*and* her royal subjects!"

Lord Tennyson licked Annie's hand affectionately, appreciative of her kindness, remembering her as a little girl, sitting with little Mary and a tiny little Ezra, all of them sharing Annie's very special Winnie-the-Pooh tea set.

Pearl petted his head and he put it on her lap. How quickly his children were growing, even just this summer. Annie was being kind and sharing—she had even apologized. Tate had taken a stand, and Pearl had acted bravely. Lord Tennyson allowed himself to stop worrying and decided he was doing a very fine job indeed.

CHAPTER ELEVEN

Mary Comes Home

LORD TENNYSON'S SENSE OF PEACE AND accomplishment lasted all the way until Saturday morning.

At last Mary was coming home! Lord Tennyson wanted to feel elated, but he felt rather ill at the inevitable sighting of the fence and the imminent reckoning between the two sisters.

News traveled so fast in the little town, it was a small miracle that the McNiffs had not seen or heard of the fence painting, due to it being a largely rainy week and Sweetums losing the phone. In addition, Mr. McNiff had been writing scene changes in his study most of the week and had not gone into town. All these factors had only dragged out the anticipation and anxiety Lord Tennyson was feeling. Because now it was certain that Annie would discover her sister's dastardly deed not while Mary was gone, but as soon as she returned.

He wondered: would Annie murder her sister in public, or wait until they arrived home?

None of the scenarios Lord Tennyson had previously pondered occurred. He hated throwing up, and the McNiff parents wanted all Mary's siblings to greet her at the bus. He, of course, had to be there. So that afternoon the McNiffs all tumbled into the truck. Lord Tennyson sat on Ezra's lap, his head out the window and his tongue wagging in the breeze to calm his nerves.

"I'm tho ekthited to thee Mary!" Tate yelled. "I mith my thithy tho much."

"Me too," Pearl said. She spoke seriously to her plastic boy. "Nicholas, did you miss Mary too?"

"Do you really think he's going to talk back?" Ezra asked.

"Mary!" Sweetums yelled, banging on her car seat. She dropped her pacifier on the floor, looked at Lord Tennyson, and then opened and closed her fist for him to fetch it.

He shook his head.

This was a game Sweetums loved to play. He knew that as soon as he gave it back to her, she would throw it again. In truth, he loved to fetch things for her, but he'd been working so hard on getting her to want to walk he was now forced to refuse.

Open and closed went her fist.

No. Lord Tennyson held firm.

She let out a howl but was soon distracted as Mr. McNiff started whistling "Man of La Mancha."

The truck snorted and sputtered as Honey drove it down the hill and along the low, flat road into town.

The sun was shining, making summer feel wonderfully lazy and hopeful.

"Almost there," Honey said. And the hopeful feeling disappeared.

Lord Tennyson panted harder as they drove closer and closer to town, closer and closer to the fence.

Meanwhile, Ezra was acting entirely too nonchalant, as if he'd completely forgotten about what Mary had done. Perhaps he had. This was just as well. Better for Ezra to be surprised than Annie suspect he was in on it.

Honey turned onto Main Street and parked a few blocks from the library so the family could enjoy a walk.

Lord Tennyson trotted beside the family without a leash, Mr. McNiff commenting on what an obedient dog he was not to run away.

He snorted at the thought. Lord Tennyson never "ran away." He did, however, sometimes take a vacation. After all, no one could be a nanny 24/7, now, could they? Today was not a vacation day, though. He stuck close by, anxious for what was coming next.

Two teenagers from the high school called out a hello to Mr. McNiff, who greatly enjoyed the attention.

"Hello there," he said. "Have you been practicing your lines for Act II? Rehearsal begins next week."

"Yes, Mr. McNiff!"

"Awesomesauce!"

"*Dad*," Annie said.

The family walked past Bellows Grocery, and Annie

peered in, no doubt looking for Cal Hubbard. Seeing school friends, she ran in to hug them instead.

"Love your outfit," Lord Tennyson heard Annie's friend Megan say.

"From Christie," Annie said excitedly.

"Like hand-me-downs? Ew."

Lord Tennyson frowned, knowing full well that everyone in town, including Megan, wanted to be a recipient of Christie Lundeen's clothes.

Annie ran back out, and all too quickly, her hurt feelings rippled into irritation with her siblings.

"Hurry up," she snapped at Tate and Pearl.

How to remind Annie that while she couldn't control Megan's words, she could control her own. Especially when it came to Mary, whom he was once again reminded of as they approached the library.

"Well, look at that. Someone has painted the fence," Honey remarked.

Lord Tennyson gulped.

"Mom, that's graffiti," Annie said impatiently.

"But it's pink graffiti, my favorite color. And look—I think it's a love poem."

"Kids, take note," Mr. McNiff remarked. "Someday you might be lucky enough to be painted about on the library fence too." He gave Honey a kiss.

"Ewwww," the children chorused.

If Ezra had forgotten what had transpired days earlier, he instantly remembered. He was suddenly walking as stiff as a robot, barely putting one foot in front of the other, his facial muscles frozen.

Sweetums clapped her hands and began squirming in her stroller.

"Out!" she yelled.

"Pink," Honey said. "Such a lovely shade of pink."

"Pink," Mr. McNiff echoed thoughtfully, as if there was something very familiar about this particular pink color.

"Yellow ith my favorite color," said Tate. "Right, Pearl?" The closer they walked, the more Annie could see. She commented on the pink swirls of flowers and large pink hearts.

"'True Love' . . ." Annie abruptly stopped walking and stared. *True Love by Old Mother Hubbard.*

"Will you read it to me?" Pearl asked.

Lord Tennyson braced himself. Annie gasped as her mother began to read.

"When I'm lonely or feeling sad, I think of you and then I'm glad. When my heart skips a beat . . . ," Honey recited.

"It *is* a love poem," Mr. McNiff said. "Well, that's one way to get someone's attention. Do you think it's a proposal?"

"Out!" Sweetums yelled again from her stroller.

Ezra's eyes became wider as he breathed faster, his chest rising and falling.

Mr. McNiff began to read the next lines.

"When I'm lonely or feeling sad, I think of you and then I'm glad . . ."

"Dad!" Annie shrieked. "Stop!"

Pearl read the letters, "C.H. + A.M."

"That rat!" Annie said.

"What?" Honey asked. "Do you know who wrote it?"

Mr. McNiff continued to read. "I feel a warm glow when we're together . . ."

His initial trepidation abandoned and finding it too funny to resist, Ezra read, "Through every high and every low. Yours forever, Mrs. Cal Hubbard."

"How romantic!" Mr. McNiff said.

Annie shrieked loudly. Lord Tennyson patted her foot with his paw, but she only had eyes for the horror before her.

Seeing them staring at the fence, the young and newly hired librarian with the cute pixie cut, Ms. Melanie Moonie, walked out to the sidewalk just as the camp bus pulled in.

"Vandalism," Ms. Melanie said, rubbing her forehead. "On my very first week."

"Romantic, poetic vandalism," Honey said.

"Our entire town should feel violated!" Mrs. Gage said, joining the group.

"Oh, we do," Mr. McNiff said solemnly.

"Unfortunately, the rain prevented us from painting over this *crime scene* the minute it happened." Ms. Melanie shook her head. "Shame it didn't wash it off."

"We can paint the fenthe!" Tate said. "I love to paint, right, Pearl?"

"We have a *lot* of pink paint," Pearl added innocently.

Ezra bit his lip.

"Maybe not pink," Ms. Melanie said. "But I'll take you up on your offer. Many hands make light work!"

The camp bus doors opened. Dirty, happy campers clambered off, chatting in excited voices.

"Mary, Mary!" Pearl and Tate jumped up and down.

"Ma-weeeeeee!" Sweetums yelled. She was so excited, she pulled out her ponytail holder and threw it on the ground.

"*Mary,*" Annie said through clenched teeth.

Ezra glanced at Lord Tennyson, barely able to suppress his laughter.

Finally, Mary bounded off the bus with her best friend, Lori. Arms entangled, they skipped over.

"We missed you so much!" Honey hugged both girls fiercely.

"It's true," Mr. McNiff said. "We nearly perished from boredom. You must never leave us again."

"Did you have fun?" Ezra asked.

"So much fun!" Mary said. "I can butterfly stroke all the way across the lake and back—I'll race you today!"

Mary was acting oblivious to the pink graffiti all over the library fence. Lord Tennyson allowed himself to hope that Mary might not acknowledge the paint and perhaps leave room for Annie to believe that someone *else* had snuck in and stolen Annie's diary while she was gone. But then, just as Lori was about to head over to her parents, Mary stopped and stared.

"Wow, look at that, Lori." Her eyes widened; her mouth dropped open. Lord Tennyson had to hand it to her. Mr. McNiff should be pleased as punch. Mary was pulling off the performance of her life. "My goodness," she gasped. "Someone spray-painted the fence! Annie . . . are those *your* initials?"

Lord Tennyson howled as loud as Sweetums.

All the way home, Mary held Lord Tennyson and chattered on and on.

"I can hold my breath for nearly two minutes!" Mary said. "I'll show you all next time at the lake."

Meanwhile, Lord Tennyson watched Annie seethe silently, staring at the back of Mary's head. At home he followed Annie as she raced up the stairs and looked in her sock drawer. Finding the key, she opened the safe.

Flipping through her diary, she paused on the Cal Hubbard parts before covering her face and hurling herself backward onto the mattress.

She sat back up and glared at him, like it was his fault, her face as angry as a hornet.

"I *know* she did it, Tenny."

It was a rare moment when Lord Tennyson was thankful he could not speak.

"When?" Annie said. "When did she paint it? That rat! That awful rat—she is *so* dead!"

Annie did not wait for an answer; nor did she put the diary back into the safe. Instead, she shoved it into her bottom drawer, under her pajamas, then stomped downstairs, where Honey was scrubbing newly harvested purple potatoes and feeding her chemistry pet with water and flour. Mary sat on the counter, happily swinging her legs. Lord Tennyson sat at her feet, on high alert. Ezra had wisely disappeared.

Mary's eyes lit up when she saw Annie.

"Hiya, Sis! Mom's making mashed taters and gravy." Mary said this so exuberantly that even Honey stopped scrubbing and looked at her strangely.

Mary rubbed her stomach and said in her most angelic voice, "Mmmm. I about starved at camp without Mom's good food."

Honey smiled at Mary. "Sweet girl! Now give me a hand," she said, handing Mary and Annie carrots and peelers.

Annie peeled vigorously, long slices of carrot falling into the compost bowl. Finally, she could take it no more. "Mary is not a sweet girl! She did it! I know she did it!"

"Did what, Sister?" Mary asked. She took the freshly peeled carrot out of Annie's hand and took a loud crunchy bite. Annie snatched it back.

"What are you talking about, Annie?" Honey asked.

"*Mary* vandalized the fence. She spray-painted the fence with *our* pink paint. It's the same color. . . ." She suddenly looked down at Lord Tennyson's head, where the few tiny spots of pink were. Her mouth fell open.

"*Annie*," Honey said. "That's just not possible. Mary was at camp."

Mary nodded, chewing loudly and looking offended by Annie's accusation. When Honey looked back at Annie, Mary stopped chewing and grinned like the Cheshire cat.

"Mary did it, I know she did it, look at her face!"

Mary opened her mouth, full of chewed-up carrots,

and suddenly looked so hurt even Lord Tennyson almost believed it.

"Annie," Honey said. "Not *everything* is Mary's fault, no matter how much you want it to be. Besides, why would she spray-paint a love poem?"

"Because she . . . I don't know how she did it, but I know she *did*."

"Do you?" Mary asked innocently, tipping her head to the side.

"Tenny!" Annie said. "If Mary did this horrible crime, nod your head up and down." He looked from one sister to the next, unsure of the best move.

Mary laughed. "That's a definite N-O."

Lord Tennyson gave her a withering look.

"Be nice to your sister, Annie," Honey scolded. "She just came home and you're already fighting."

"I can't be nice to her when she spray-paints words. . . ."

"What words do you mean?" Mary asked, dripping with sweetness. "Say which ones."

Annie glared at her, bursting to explain, but again she stopped abruptly. Lord Tennyson was sympathetic. She couldn't admit that she had actually written a poem entitled "True Love" about Cal Hubbard without severe mortification. He gave her a loving lick, pleading for peace, while Mary silently cackled.

Peace was on neither sister's agenda.

Lord Tennyson wondered how on earth he was going to prevent World War III from taking over the house now.

CHAPTER TWELVE

Mrs. Gage Is Deathly Afraid of Snakes

THE FENCE WAS PAINTED A BRIGHT WHITE
(*NOT pink!*) as a service project the next week. The entire
McNiff family helped paint, including Sweetums, until she
began painting Lord Tennyson and he had to put her in a
wheelbarrow. The refreshed fence was a facelift to the entire
town, and most especially the library, but it did nothing
to melt the frost between the sisters. Even Honey and Mr.
McNiff seemed irritable at the tension, but Lord Tennyson

could see no way to soften their hearts toward one another.

"Children," Honey said one warm night in July. "Tomorrow your father and I are going out of town on a costume hunt. We expect you to be kind and take care of each other." She looked pointedly at Annie and Mary, who were barely speaking. "Follow your chore chart and get all your work done before you play. And take care of the pets."

Lord Tennyson wondered if he had forgotten about this trip or if Honey and Mr. McNiff had forgotten to consult him. He scratched his ear, already making a bedtime plan for the younger McNiffs. Felicity and Delilah hopped past him. Now, *those* animals were pets. They hadn't a thought in their head except to hop, chew, and poo. They were almost potty-trained in a small plastic tray in the laundry room, but occasionally they left behind small black pellets. Like now. He sniffed them, a combined scent of grass and bunny chow. He'd like to see these bunny creatures raise humans. Ha!

Mr. McNiff leaned forward to see what Lord Tennyson was sniffing.

"What," Mr. McNiff said, his nose close to a black pellet on the ground, "is *that*?"

Silence.

"Is that . . . ?"

"Bunny pellet poo," Tate said.

"Excellent fertilizer," Honey added.

"You mean to tell me we have rabbits hopping around the house *pooing* on our floors?"

"They're mothtly potty-trained, not like Thweetums," Tate said.

Hearing her name, Sweetums banged on her high-chair tray. Hearing Sweetums, the bunnies wisely scurried under the couch.

"Children," Honey said, trying to get them back on track. "While we are gone, we'd like you to remember it takes all of us to keep a home running smoothly."

Mr. McNiff, trying to forget about the bunny pellets, said, "Let us recall the analogy of pedaling the family bike all together. Each one of you is responsible for—"

There was a collective groan from everyone except Lord Tennyson, who was enjoying Mr. McNiff patting his head.

"Why do you have to leave?" Pearl said with a frown. "What if something happens?"

"Happens?" Mr. McNiff said. "What could happen?

You have Lord Tennyson to protect you! Anyway, we have to go. Dulcinea, our lead actress, is in desperate need of something suitable to wear."

"And!" Honey said. "Mrs. Gage will be coming over to check on you so you won't be alone."

"Not Mrs. Gage!" Ezra said.

"She can't even see!" Annie said. "Whoever heard of hiring a blind babysitter?"

"Plus, she despises us," Mary added.

"I'm sure that's not true," Honey said.

Actually, it was true. Also understandable, if you did not know and love the McNiff children the way Lord Tennyson did.

Normally, he liked and admired the classy and strict Mrs. Gage, even though she was the owner of Fat Cat. It was true that she was ancient and had lost nearly all her sight, but Mrs. Gage was exactly the type of well-mannered example Lord Tennyson normally approved of.

Normally.

But what possible reason could Honey and Mr. McNiff have for asking Mrs. Gage to check on the children with Lord Tennyson at the helm? Were they *still* losing faith in him? He had not heard any rumblings of a "real nanny" or "more help" in the last few weeks, thanks to his tireless efforts. He was getting older, but just mere minutes ago hadn't he been praised as their protector? Furthermore, he could still hear and *see*!

Yet as he looked at the children, he decided to hope for the best. Perhaps Mrs. Gage's very mannerly presence would help the children snap out of their latest, trying phase.

Before he and Honey left the next day, Mr. McNiff pulled Annie and Mary aside.

"Remember . . ."

"Pedal the bike," they said in unison. But when he turned around, Mary looked cross-eyed at Annie behind her cat-eyed glasses and Annie stuck her tongue out.

At the doorway, Honey bent down to rub Lord Tennyson's neck. "Be safe," she said, kissing him on the nose. He gazed into Honey's eyes and put his nose to hers. Oh yes, he would do anything for his beloved Honey.

"Help them," Mr. McNiff said to him this time, "to pedal together?"

Lord Tennyson saluted with a firm nod of his head, more determined than ever.

But Lord Tennyson hardly had a chance to do anything, because Mrs. Gage didn't simply check in.

She *moved* in, arriving on their driveway with her large turquoise suitcase that looked remarkably like bright blue snakeskin. She also carried a small overnight bag filled with creams and an exorbitant amount of medicine. (He knew this because Sweetums had once managed to open a bottle and eat all the "candy" on a previous visit, which resulted in a lively exchange with Poison Control.) As always, Mrs. Gage was in full makeup that was overly done, likely due to her failing eyesight. Around her neck was her oversized magnifying glass.

Making matters worse was the furball slinking up behind her: Fat Cat had come too.

She meowed a smug greeting to Lord Tennyson while curling herself around Mrs. Gage.

"Therpenth are cold-blooded, legleth, carnivorouth reptileth," Tate said, seeing the suitcase. "They can be dithtinguithed from legleth lithardth by their lack of eyelidth."

"How the heck do you know that?" Annie asked.

"Sh!" Ezra said, elbowing his younger brother.

Mrs. Gage shuddered. "Oh, please don't talk about those abhorrent creatures." Her wrinkly pink lips frowned.

"That lookth like Ethra'th thnake," Tate said, pointing to the suitcase. "Ekthept it'th blue."

Ezra forced a laugh and clapped his hand around Tate's mouth, whispering, "Shut it, she hates snakes!"

"Uh, Ethra?" Tate said. "I have thumthing to tell you."

"Later!" Ezra said.

Lord Tennyson eyed Tate sharply.

Mere minutes ago, he had discovered Tate petting Snake without Ezra's permission. Feeling bolder since successfully learning to ride the bike, Tate had helped Snake take a walk around the room. Unfortunately, Snake was very fast and had slithered into a small crack in the closet. For Tate's sake, Lord Tennyson hoped Snake would find his way back to his home in the cardboard box.

But he momentarily forgot about Tate's snake secret when Mrs. Gage's attention finally settled on her favorite McNiff family member.

"There's that dashing miniature schnauzer!" she cooed, bringing up her magnifying glass to admire his beard and whiskers, which Mr. McNiff had brushed before leaving. "Aren't you the most majestic dog in the world?"

He beamed, so pleased by her attention that he was almost able to overlook the purpose of her being here.

Sweetums ended the moment by pulling on his stubby tail, mortifying him in front of the distinguished Mrs. Gage, as well as Fat Cat, who enjoyed his humiliation far too much.

Avoiding Sweetums (who was picked up by Mary) and his nemesis, Lord Tennyson trotted beside Mrs. Gage up the driveway, admiring her lavender-rinsed hair and her fastidious ensemble. Resigned to her presence, he hoped her fine civility would rub off on the children and that she would give an excellent report to Honey and Mr. McNiff.

But Sweetums suddenly crumbled. "Mamaaaa!"

"What's this?" Mrs. Gage asked, leaning over, looking through her magnifying glass. The children giggled because when Mrs. Gage held the magnifying glass in front of her eye, she looked a lot like a one-eyed monster.

"Sut up!" Sweetums said.

This was one of those rare moments when Mrs. Gage's near deafness worked in the children's favor.

"What did you say, dear?"

Annie plucked Sweetums from Mary's arms. "Oh, nothing."

"Sut up!" Sweetums yelled.

"One more time." Mrs. Gage came closer with her giant eye.

"She said, 'Shut up,'" Mary offered loudly, annoyed with Annie for taking the baby.

"Oh my!" Mrs. Gage frowned at Sweetums, who buried her face and runny nose into Annie's neck.

Lord Tennyson nudged Mrs. Gage inside. Before Fat Cat could enter, he turned and glared to indicate she was unwelcome, but she was already disappearing behind the hosta bushes.

Once inside, he cringed. He had overseen the cleaning before Mrs. Gage's arrival himself! In the minutes he'd been looking for Snake, the living room had become a disaster that Mrs. Gage would be able to see even without her magnifying glass.

The cushions were strewn about from a pillow fight. Toys and books were scattered on the floor, and a lamp was balancing precariously on the ledge of a scuffed-up end table. Polly Pockets, Legos, and doll accessories suddenly littered the steps leading upstairs, while Pearl's Nicholas doll was hanging by floss from the light fixture. Combined with the sagging couch, the stained striped chair, and the small holes poked into the curtains that had looked new a year ago, this was not the first impression he wanted.

"Nicholas!" Pearl cried happily, seeing him swinging in the air.

Mrs. Gage opened her eyes very wide.

"Let's pedal the bike," Annie said, feeling chagrined by the mess.

"Why?" Mary said. "Mom and Dad aren't here."

Mrs. Gage's giant eye came to rest on Mary. "Rather than bike riding, we should be tidying this living room. Go on now."

Sulking, Mary began gathering puzzle pieces. Annie put Sweetums down on the couch, wiped her nose (and her own neck), and ordered Pearl and Tate to organize the books they had dumped on the floor. When she bent down to help them, Lord Tennyson felt a surge of hope. Here they were, pedaling the family bike! Feeling generous, he allowed that perhaps the respectable Mrs. Gage was a useful reinforcement to his own skills. Only a reinforcement. Nothing more.

Lord Tennyson laid his nose on Annie's arm as a show of approval that she was using her older-sibling powers for good.

Sweetums sat on the couch, no longer wailing but looking very cross.

"Tenny, I think it's naptime for the baby," Ezra said.

He was right. Lord Tennyson trotted over to the couch so Sweetums could slide on and he could carry her upstairs.

"Well, isn't that cute!" Mrs. Gage cooed.

"Not cute!" Sweetums yelled. "You not cute!"

Sweetums had not taken the bike analogy to heart and was more of a "push the bike over" kind of toddler.

Mrs. Gage took a step back, startled, but unfortunately, Mary was behind her on her hands and knees, looking for the last puzzle pieces under a chair.

Mrs. Gage toppled backward over Mary and landed with a large thud on the soft armchair.

The room became very, very still.

"Ith she dead?!" Tate asked.

Lord Tennyson and the children scrambled over to Mrs. Gage.

"Mrs. Gage?" Annie asked softly. "Are you . . . alive?"

Mrs. Gage struggled upright and fluffed her lavender-colored hair.

"I'm fine, children. I'm fine. Let me gather myself together again."

When Sweetums vaguely and crossly swatted at Mrs. Gage, Lord Tennyson pivoted quickly and carried the soft baby lump up the stairs, one step at a time. His joints felt every step as Sweetums clung to his hair. He was getting too old for this—not that Mrs. Gage was any younger!

He stepped over a dirty sock, a pair of underwear (without even stopping to sniff), and an old toothbrush. Finally, just as he thought Sweetums might pull his ears right off, they made it to her crib. This was not where she took her naps, however.

Lord Tennyson nudged Sweetums off onto the soft nap pillow on the floor. He pulled a blanket over her with his teeth. Thankfully, Sweetums did not object. Instead, she put her thumb in her mouth and waited. Lord Tennyson trotted back to the bedroom door and, using his nose, shut the door tightly. He came back to Sweetums and her big blue eyes, still shiny with tears. She was the only McNiff child with eyes the exact color of Honey's blueberries. Sweetums's eyelids blinked wet, dark lashes as she pulled him closer.

"No nap," she said. "No!"

He stared at her, and she relented, closing her eyes.

Lord Tennyson nestled into her, and within minutes both of them were snoring softly. It was even better than a nap under the lilac bush.

By the time he and Sweetums awoke, the house was just the way Honey and Mr. McNiff liked it, and even Sweetums was more pleasant. Mrs. Gage had apparently recovered in time to oversee the cleaning of the kitchen. As far as Lord Tennyson knew, Osbert hadn't put up a fight. Lord Tennyson wanted to enjoy the clean kitchen but was starting to feel that Mrs. Gage's presence was a bit too effective.

They ate a polite dinner together, with Mrs. Gage eating out of a container filled with something she called "Kale Surprise."

"Mama would like that," Pearl said. "She loves kale!"

"This kale is from your very own garden!" Mrs. Gage said. The children beamed with admiration that their mother could produce something Mrs. Gage would eat.

"I don't know how your mother does it, but her vegetables grow bigger and better than anyone's I know."

"It'th cock-a-doodle-poo," Tate said, quoting his mother. "A farmer'th betht friend."

"Pardon?" Mrs. Gage asked, cupping her ear.

"Poo," Sweetums said.

"Fertilizer," Annie corrected.

"Pooooo!" Sweetums yelled.

Mary and Ezra snorted with laughter.

Mrs. Gage sniffed and shuddered. "Yes," she said dryly. "This house has a particular . . . odor."

It certainly did. Lord Tennyson sniffed his way over to the chick box, which now sat atop the washing machine. Their smell was getting more potent by the day.

"Has anyone fed Tenny?" Ezra asked.

At the mention of food, Lord Tennyson dashed back to the table and parked himself underneath Sweetums's chair.

"Napkins, children," Mrs. Gage said, shaking out a white napkin and laying it carefully on her lap.

"Yes, napkins, children," Annie said, as if it were perfectly natural to eat dinner with white napkins on their laps.

Sweetums threw a wet, curly noodle at him.

Lord Tennyson didn't have a white napkin on his lap, but he ate it anyway.

As far as a McNiff dinner went, it was a great success, with no major spills or meltdowns. After dinner, Annie said, "Thank you for coming over."

Lord Tennyson had lined the children up by the front door with the expectation that each would utter their sincere thanks. He was also prepared to prod Ezra and Mary to walk Mrs. Gage home.

"Thank you for having me!" Mrs. Gage said, holding up her magnifying glass. "Now, where shall my sweet kitty and I sleep? Here, kitty, kitty." A loud meow came from outside the front door.

Lord Tennyson paused mid-paw-shake.

"Sleep?" Mary asked, alarmed.

Kitty?

"You aren't thpending the night," Tate said. "You're jutht checking in with uth."

"What? And leave you children all alone?" Mrs. Gage said loudly.

"We have Lord Tennyson," Ezra said.

Mrs. Gage smiled. "Oh, darlings, he's just a *dog*."

Lord Tennyson blinked, aghast, *betrayed*.

"Well?" Mrs. Gage asked.

"Uh, you can sleep here," Annie said to Mrs. Gage, patting the couch. "We'll get the little ones ready for bed."

Mrs. Gage bent over the couch with her magnifying glass, squinting for signs of filth. To make matters far worse, Tate opened the front door and in walked Fat Cat. In her mouth was Sweetums's pacifier, which she'd found under the hosta bush.

"Mine!" Sweetums yelled.

Lord Tennyson barked at the allergenic puffball to walk herself back out, but Mrs. Gage scolded him into silence.

"Oh, my darling!" Mrs. Gage said, picking Fat Cat up and wrapping her around her neck. Safe in the arms of Mrs. Gage, Fat Cat smugly sucked on the pacifier.

There was nothing to be done but lift his chin and march past her without acknowledgment, even when she flicked her hairy tail at him. Lord Tennyson would be sure that Mr. McNiff and Honey heard about this!

"Mine!" Sweetums yowled all the way up to her room.

With Lord Tennyson supervising, Annie, Mary, and Ezra assisted their buddies by helping them brush their teeth, putting their pajamas on, reading them a story, and fetching small drinks of water. Lord Tennyson herded the children back and forth from the bathroom while enduring more good-night hugs than usual, particularly from Pearl, who kept looking sadly at her parents' empty bedroom.

The oldest siblings kissed their younger siblings good night, tucked them all into Pearl's double bed, and finally closed the door behind them. Mary leaned against the doorframe and said, "That was exhausting!" Which, Lord Tennyson had to admit, was gratifying.

Mrs. Gage's loud snoring could already be heard from downstairs, and immediately, Lord Tennyson's self-confidence was restored.

It was at that moment they heard a faraway howling outside, across the fields.

"Aah!" Pearl yelled from the bedroom. "It's the wolves. They're eating our Tenny boy!"

171

Ezra opened the door again.

"Our boy is right here!"

Lord Tennyson quickly trotted in, uneaten, but kept his ears alert to the coyote howls. Sometimes they were so loud it sounded like they were just outside the bedroom door. He barked in return for them to stop scaring his Pearl.

"Now, listen," Ezra said. "Go to sleep. There are no wolves."

"But I can hear them," Pearl wailed.

"Are they in the clothet?" Tate asked, worried.

"They're far, far away outside," Mary said. "Now go to sleep."

Sweetums let out a loud howl that sounded more like a strangled chicken.

"We should say our prayers," Annie said.

"To keep the woofth away," Tate said.

Lord Tennyson nodded his approval and barked once more, but then he caught a scent. Nose to the ground, he began sniffing. Just last week there had been an unidentifiable paw print in the backyard, and missing chickens reported from Mr. Goody's! The children had first blamed Lord Tennyson, but he had assured them that if he had

172

eaten a chicken, they would have known. Were Pearl and Tate's worries accurate?

"What is it, boy?" Ezra asked. Tate, Pearl, Nicholas, and Sweetums sat up in bed.

"Ezra, prayer!" Annie ordered.

"Say thank you first!" Mary whispered.

Ezra prayed, first thanking God for Lord Tennyson.

Lord Tennyson stopped sniffing a moment to agree he was a blessing.

"And . . . we are thankful for our house even though it's pink and for our car even though it's always broken and for good food to eat even if it's vegetables and for our parents who . . . are away and we miss them."

The children sniffed.

"Please bless them to come home safely . . . and please bless that the wolves stay away tonight! Amen." The littles opened their eyes, looking even more frightened than before.

Mary gave her siblings a kiss on the cheek.

"Nicholas too," Pearl said, holding him up.

"I'm not kissing Nicholas."

"*I'll* do it," Annie said. She kissed Nicholas and his coifed plastic hair at the same time Mary whispered, "Oh, Cal!"

Annie elbowed Mary while Pearl hugged Nicholas to her, pleased. Lord Tennyson wanted to address the bickering, but the scent drew him back to sniffing the ground, stopping in the corners, and smelling in between the small cracks in the floor. He suddenly knew what the scent was. It was not a wolf or a coyote. It was athe scent of . . . Snake.

A half hour later Lord Tennyson was still sniffing in the dark, his nails clicking on the ground. *Sniff, sniff, Snake . . .*

He sniffed all the way down the hall and back again to where Mary was wandering into Ezra's room. Ezra sat on his bed reading.

Mary looked at Lord Tennyson, then peered into Ezra's secret snake box, moving the grass around the cardboard box and picking up the water dish.

"Ezra?"

"Mmmm?"

"Where is Snake?"

"He's there," Ezra said, not taking his eyes off his book.

"No, he's not!" Mary said as Annie came in brushing her teeth.

Annie froze, then jumped onto Ezra's bed, forcing him to look up.

"A snake?" Annie demanded, her mouth covered with white toothpaste. "Why?!"

"For a pet, of course." Ezra got up and looked into the box. "Ah man, he really did it. He escaped!"

Lord Tennyson picked up a scent from under Ezra's bed. He wriggled until he was all the way underneath the bed in the dark.

"Did you take it?" Annie asked Mary accusingly.

"Why would I take it?" Mary said. "Unless . . . I wanted to put it under your pillow. Maybe it's there now."

"Mary!" Annie yelled.

Lord Tennyson growled for them to quiet down so he could focus.

"Oh hush, you scaredy-cat," Mary hissed. "Ezra, where *is* the snake? It can't just slither around the house."

"I don't know!" Ezra said. "He's just gone."

Lord Tennyson stuck his head out from under the bed. Annie turned pale, eyes scanning the ground. Lord Tennyson thought he had best find Snake before she became hysterical.

"We just have to hope Snake keeps going wherever he's going," Mary said. "And that he doesn't get discovered under Mrs. Gage's magnifying glass. She'd definitely tell Mom and Dad."

That night, before going to bed, the elder McNiff children double-checked the insides of their covers before getting in. The thought of a slithering snake wiggling across their feet or faces during the night kept them all in a fitful sleep. As for Lord Tennyson, he didn't sleep a wink. Sensing calamity, and being an exceptionally responsible nanny, he knew that he must find that snake before the parents heard one word of it.

CHAPTER THIRTEEN

Good Night, Lavinia

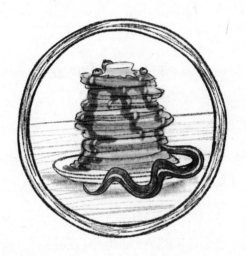

"THNAKEY DID NOT COME BACK TO HITH LITTLE houth!"

Lord Tennyson awoke with a start to see Tate standing next to him. It wasn't often that a McNiff child was awake before he was, but he was still drowsy after spending half the night sniffing out Snake, without success, as Tate noted.

Frightened of a nighttime Snake encounter, Annie,

Mary, and Ezra had all ended up in Ezra's bed, tighter than sardines. Annie raised her head up.

"Have you seen Snake, Tatey?"

"Yethterday. When I thtroked his thlithery cold-blooded thnake thkin."

Mary opened her eyes. "You let him out?"

Tate opened his eyes wide and splayed out his fingers. "He jutht thlithered from my hand."

"Tate!" both sisters said at the same time. Lord Tennyson watched them look at each other in surprise, as if they couldn't believe they actually agreed on something. How refreshing!

"Where did he go?" Annie demanded, sitting up.

"Into the depth of Ethra's clothet, where the woofth live."

"For the thousandth time, wolves don't live in the closet!" Annie said. But to double-check, they tiptoed to Ezra's closet and peered in.

"He'th gone!" Tate said, beginning to cry. "The woof ate him!"

"Tate," Ezra said, yawning. "There are no wolves in there. I was just joking that one time." Lord Tennyson shook his head. Children did *not* forget this kind of joke.

"They come out at night if I don't go to thleep," Tate said. "Mary thed."

Mary suddenly became preoccupied with her fingernails.

To change the subject, Lord Tennyson stood, stretched his joints, and motioned for the children to follow him downstairs. They filled his bowls with water and food and let him outside immediately. He was most proud of this progress.

While having a loop around the yard, with a stop at his favorite birch tree, Lord Tennyson saw Fat Cat crouched on the stone wall in the backyard. The pacifier was gone from her mouth. Instead, she had her eye on a bird. He paused to watch, but the bird flew away before Fat Cat could pounce. Amateur! He sniffed on his way back inside the house to see if Snake had found his way back to the yard, but instead he picked up the smell of breakfast.

Mrs. Gage was standing in the kitchen humming, stirring pancake batter. On the counter were chocolate chips and blueberries. His mouth watered. Annie was smiling, until she froze as still as a stone.

Lord Tennyson followed her gaze.

Snake.

He was inching his way along the counter, blending into the countertop, and settled close to the spatula Mrs. Gage was absently reaching for. For one fascinating and delicious moment Lord Tennyson imagined Mrs. Gage grabbing Snake and tossing him into the pancake batter. He licked his beard: Snake pancakes.

Annie didn't have the same wonderful anticipation on her face.

"Good morning, my fine gentleman," Mrs. Gage said, her pinkie finger brushing up against Snake as she picked up the spatula and stirred blueberries into batter. Snake coiled up into a ball and didn't move. Lord Tennyson barked and jumped up, panting.

"Now, now," Mrs. Gage said. "Hold your horses. Breakfast is coming!"

Annie opened her mouth but thought better of it.

Snake uncurled and inched his way closer to Mrs. Gage's bowl, his little slip of tongue darting in and out. Taking a deep breath and biting her lip, Annie lunged bravely for Snake but succeeded only in getting dangerously close to knocking Osbert off the counter. Snake disappeared behind a blue-and-white-checkered bowl.

"And you, dearie," Mrs. Gage said. "You can hold your horses too! Call your brothers and sisters down, and we'll sit at the table for breakfast."

Annie nodded and ran upstairs. Lord Tennyson sat with his eyes fixated on Snake coiled behind the bowl. Behind him, Fat Cat slowly meowed. Just what he needed, a tattletale.

Once the children were downstairs, Lord Tennyson was forced to abandon Snake watch to help with breakfast. With the exception of Annie, who still looked slightly panicked and pale, the McNiff children devoured breakfast with the ferocity of uncouth animals, eager to eat their fill before a sibling got more than their share. Lord Tennyson wondered if all big families were like this, where food was such a prized possession that each meal was practically a sporting event. At least Lord Tennyson was happily full. In addition to his dog kibble, Mrs. Gage had given him a piece of bacon and he had cleaned up the multiple bites of pancakes that Sweetums had either thrown or dropped. His beard was satisfyingly sticky with maple syrup. So far, though, no Snake pancakes.

The children's appetites delighted Mrs. Gage, who glowed at every greedy gobble. Ezra and Mary kept looking at each other, trying to keep from laughing as Annie carefully inspected both sides of her pancakes before taking a single bite.

"Today'th the day!" Tate said, bouncing up and down on the bench. "Dad thed the chickenth go outthide."

"What's that, dear?" Mrs. Gage asked, lifting her magnifying glass.

"The chicks are old enough to live outside with the flock now," Ezra said. "Dad will be happy, because they stink." He plugged his nose.

Lord Tennyson looked up in alarm. The time had passed so quickly! He would have to say a proper good-bye to the chicks and their wonderful aroma. He trotted over to the washing machine and sat below the box atop it, then inhaled deeply. Oh, it was glorious.

Fat Cat suddenly appeared, slinking by and jumping onto the washing machine. She taunted him by meowing and then, paw by paw, approached the box with the chicks inside.

Lord Tennyson barked a warning. Tempting as they were, the children's chicks were *not* for eating!

Fat Cat ignored him, putting her paws on the rim of the box and peering in, her eyes following their every move.

Lord Tennyson barked more insistently, running back and forth until the children jumped up from breakfast and came running.

"Grab the cat!" Pearl screamed.

"Oh dear, oh dear, sweet kitty," Mrs. Gage said, reaching for Fat Cat and lifting her off the washing machine. "We don't eat these birdies." She turned to the McNiffs. "It's best if the chicks could go sooner rather than later. Fat Cat *is* a cat after all." Lord Tennyson noted the injustice of this statement, as she had declared him "just a dog" and he was the one with self-control. Mrs. Gage opened the door, and out Fat Cat went.

The children surrounded the chicks in their box.

"That wath a clothe call!" Tate announced.

Pearl exhaled in relief. Lord Tennyson tried his best not to salivate.

But Fat Cat's attempt had made it harder, reminding him of their deliciousness. How much self-control could one distinguished schnauzer be expected to have? The chicks had been there for six weeks and were now big enough to hop and fly. Their yellow feet taunted him. He could almost *taste* a delicious bird in his mouth. He could *feel* his whole body quivering with excitement.

Right at that moment, one of the yellow chicks flew out of the box and perched on the edge.

"It's Lavinia!" Annie said proudly.

Lord Tennyson's heartbeat quickened; his tongue fell out, and he stood on his back legs for a better look, whining with barely suppressed pleasure.

"Come on now," Annie said. "Let's go outside to the chicken coop."

He began to follow, but Annie put her hand out.

"Ezra, hold him. Don't, under any circumstances, let Tenny outside until the chicks are safely in the coop."

Well! Lord Tennyson was very taken aback. *How rude!*

Ezra shut the screen door after Pearl, Tate, and Sweetums followed their big sisters out to the backyard. They watched as Annie and Mary set the box down on the lawn.

"Look at their cute and cuddly bird featherth," Tate said, reaching out to touch Lavinia.

Sweetums took Lavinia, her chubby hands somewhat

soft for once. Lavinia fluttered loose and perched on Sweetums's shoulder.

Lord Tennyson was going to turn away to temper the temptation, but then he saw something that made his heart race even faster—Fat Cat again. Lurking behind the crab apple tree.

"Steady, boy," Ezra said, his hand around Lord Tennyson's collar.

"Edith," Tate breathed, stroking a bird before setting her down in the grass.

The six chickens hobbled around on the lawn. With their new freedom, they darted this way and that. Annie shrieked for the children to herd them toward the coop before they ran away. They did as she asked, all except for Sweetums. She crawled over to the crab apple tree with Lavinia still perched on her shoulder. Little did she know that she was headed straight toward Fat Cat. Lord Tennyson scratched at the door to be let out immediately!

"Mine," Sweetums said.

Mrs. Gage joined Lord Tennyson and Ezra, looking out the screen door.

"How adorable," she said, holding up her magnifying

glass to get a better look. At that moment, Lord Tennyson and Mrs. Gage spied something at the very same time: something long and black curling toward them on the floor. Mrs. Gage screamed so loudly the windowpanes rattled. She reached for the door handle.

"No!" Ezra started. But it was too late. Mrs. Gage flung open the door and ran outside yelling, "SNAKE!"

The back door was open.

Lord Tennyson bolted out of Ezra's grasp. Chickens were on the loose, and he would save them from Fat Cat!

Screaming, the children dropped the chicks back into the box and assumed ninjalike poses, holding out their arms to keep Lord Tennyson at bay. He wanted to tell them he was not the enemy; Fat Cat was!

The children began chasing him, trying to catch and grab him.

Lord Tennyson was enraptured by this game, instantly remembering how Mr. McNiff had circled the table and tried to catch a chicken. How scared he'd been. Just watch how easily Lord Tennyson could do it! He felt younger than he had in years, running this way and that as he tried to get to Sweetums and Lavinia.

But then Lady Mary flapped her feathers and flew out of the box, perching atop Tate's head and pulling Lord Tennyson's focus.

"Aah!" Tate yelled. "Chicken on my head!"

"Don't move," Annie commanded. "Don't move an inch or Tenny will eat her!"

Eat her! No . . . but oh, the thought was a terrific one.

Mary rescued Lady Mary from Tate's head, and Lord Tennyson resumed his focus on Lavinia and Fat Cat, feeling no stiffness in his knees as he ran through the obstacle course of children.

"Mine," he heard Sweetums say.

They turned to see Sweetums still holding Lavinia under the crab apple tree. And who should be making her move but Fat Cat, as predicted. She glanced at Lord Tennyson and smiled a slow, wicked smile. Then she fixed her eyes on Lavinia and began to silently tiptoe around the tree. Very cunning and *catlike*.

Lord Tennyson gave up the game and dashed toward Sweetums.

Ezra and Mary chased after him.

"Thweetums! Hold the chicken," Tate hollered.

"Mine!" she yelled, putting her hands out to show them.

Lord Tennyson was getting closer and closer. So was Fat Cat.

But with one flying leap, Ezra tackled him.

"Help him, Mary," Annie said, panicky. "Grab Tenny!" No one said anything about the cat—couldn't they see what was about to happen?

"I will save the chicken!" Pearl screamed.

Pearl's unexpected declaration surprised Ezra enough that he lost his grip just as she lunged for a wiggling Lord Tennyson, letting him slip from both children's grasps.

"Mine!" Sweetums demanded, standing up and taking one wobbly step that in any other moment would have filled him with pride. But seeing Lord Tennyson charging, she plopped back down.

Fat Cat paused midstep, and Lord Tennyson felt pure exhilaration as he charged forward.

Everything else faded. Even Fat Cat. He only had eyes for Lavinia.

What had started as a rescue mission had transformed into something else. All he could see was *bird*. All he could

hear were little *cheeping* sounds. All he could smell was chicken poo—glorious chicken poo!

Sweetums was on the move now, crawling quickly with the bird balanced precariously on her shoulder. Fat Cat's pause had been enough. Lord Tennyson got to Sweetums first, running circles around her, inching closer and closer.

"Sweetums," Ezra warned. "Give me the chick."

Sweetums only crawled faster in the opposite direction.

"Oh no," Annie whispered. "Please no."

"Stop the doggy," Mrs. Gage said, standing on the back porch and waving her magnifying glass. "Stop that doggy." Her face was flushed as if she felt the great weight of her actions, the perilous danger the chicks were now in. Even though she called him "doggy," she had opened the back door. Lord Tennyson would love her the rest of his life.

Ezra assumed a defensive stance in front of Lord Tennyson. "Stay," he said in his firmest voice. Lord Tennyson may have obeyed this command had Sweetums not suddenly reached down and put Lavinia on the grass. The chicken pecked and took a few steps as Sweetums laughed and clapped her hands.

"Mine."

But Sweetums was wrong; this chicken was Lord Tennyson's. Sweetums let out a great shriek as he descended. He felt feathers tickle his nose as he opened his mouth and . . .

What self-satisfied delight he felt as his eyes met Fat Cat's. *He* had won Lavinia from a far less worthy pursuer!

"No!" Pearl screamed, grabbing him. She shook him and the chicken fell from his mouth. Fat Cat was coming toward them once again. Lavinia toddled away, slightly dazed. Tate scooped her up off the ground.

He could almost hear the children and Mrs. Gage exhale.

But this was premature.

He was Lord Tennyson, a rather spectacular dog. Didn't the children see that the chick would never be safe with Fat Cat around? And if anyone deserved a tasty treat, wasn't it him?

He moved left and then right. He ran through Pearl's legs, bounding forward and circling back until he was in front of Tate. He did something he never did—he jumped on Tate.

"Ah!" Tate yelled. "Hith teeth are terrifying!"

And Lavinia was once again on the ground.

He snatched Lavinia into his mouth, and this time he made a run for it, far from the interfering children and the cat.

Chaos ensued. The children collectively screamed and Pearl sobbed.

He hid under the forsythia bush with his winnings as the children disappeared back into the house with the other five chicks.

"We're prisoners in our own house!" Lord Tennyson heard Mary moan. "We'll never be able to go outside again!"

"It's not for forever," Ezra said. "I mean, there's just not that much chicken. . . ."

"Stop it, Ezzie. Stop it!" Pearl sobbed harder.

"But that's what dogs do. They eat birds."

Lord Tennyson was glad to have a defender, but then suddenly, he heard a familiar voice.

"What's all this?" Mr. McNiff asked.

The children begin yelling and crying once again.

Lord Tennyson raced to the back door, where Mr. McNiff and Honey were standing.

He saw the six children crying on the kitchen floor and Mrs. Gage huddled by the sink, distraught. For the first time since the chase had begun he started to feel something other than chicken delight.

"Tenny!"

"He's so mean!"

"I'll never forgive him."

"How could he?!"

"MINE!"

"What's . . . in his mouth?" Honey asked.

The parents peered closer.

"Come here, boy. What have you got?" Mr. McNiff said.

Lord Tennyson trotted closer, greatly wanting to impress Mr. McNiff. He was almost in the back door when Mr. McNiff's eyes became wide with revulsion as he saw two limp yellow legs, bobbing up and down and hitting Lord Tennyson's salt-and-pepper goatee.

"He *mortally wounded* Lavinia!" Tate said, the tears flowing.

"AHHHHHH!" Mr. McNiff yelled, practically pushing Lord Tennyson out the back door. "Out, out, out!"

Rejected by his great hero, his ears and whole body

drooped. He took his prized bird to the front yard, where Mrs. Gage was exiting quickly. She gasped and dropped her magnifying glass.

"There is something very wrong with *that dog.*" *Not to mention the children!* she left unsaid. Lord Tennyson deflated, no longer feeling anywhere near majestic in her eyes.

"Mrs. Gage—thank you so much—" Honey called after her. But Mrs. Gage was gone down the road, her turquoise snakeskin suitcase flying after her. Waddling behind her was Fat Cat, tail high in the air, both salty that it was Lord Tennyson who had gotten the bird and smug that no one liked him anymore.

He felt a glimmer of hope when Mary, though angry, began to defend him.

"There is nothing wrong with our Tenny! NOTH-ING!" Mary yelled. But when Lord Tennyson trotted back toward the house to thank her, she screamed and ran away. Suddenly his victory didn't taste as heavenly.

CHAPTER FOURTEEN

A Funeral Procession

THE DAY AFTER MRS. GAGE LEFT, THE CHILDREN WERE still hesitant to go outside. Who knew what bird remains they would encounter? At first Lord Tennyson felt a bit triumphant that things hadn't exactly ended on a peaceful note with another caretaker in the house. In fact, they'd ended worse!

Triumph soon soured. Although the children had been fed, followed the chore chart, and gone to bed on time, all his good work was now overshadowed by what would forever be referred to as "the chicken incident." His determination to show the parents his excellent child-minding ways was all for naught. Mr. McNiff's impressive Pedaling the Family Bike analogy was now far away in the rearview mirror. Ezra's pet snake was on the loose, children were crying, and Mrs. Gage had left in a huff—his reputation was tarnished worse than before!

No one mentioned Fat Cat. No, all fault fell squarely on Lord Tennyson's gentlemanly shoulders. Though Mrs. Gage and the children *had* played a part, he knew he must take full responsibility, as he had always taught the children they should when it came to their choices and actions.

No one had *made* him eat Lavinia.

He could hardly even explain it himself now that the high of the chase had worn off.

He, who was always so in control of himself, who was always so measured and wise . . . had eaten the children's bird.

He remembered the day Mr. McNiff had caught a chick. He had not eaten it. What had stopped him? Fear? But Lord Tennyson was not afraid of birds.

Proud of his dog heritage, he was also a nanny and knew he must not let the natural dog in him take over at inappropriate times. Though he loved birds, he must not eat the children's chickens, only birds that were not named. Never again could he let Fat Cat's taunting motivate him in any way.

Surely he had given Honey and Mr. McNiff reason to further doubt his abilities.

This seemed to be confirmed as Mr. McNiff and Honey approached him all morning with hesitancy, as if they were afraid of him—or of what might be lingering in his mouth. And the children! Oh, the children were holding a grudge. Finally, they had united against a common enemy—but that enemy was Lord Tennyson!

It was a day of much sorrow and moping. Finally, after lunch, Honey shooed the children outside, and Lord Tennyson was determined to make up with them. He dropped a ball at their feet. Might they want to play fetch? But no, they let the ball sit sadly on the ground, not even attempting to chase it. He was surprised by how much he missed their noise and rambunctious affection.

He picked the ball up again and dropped it in Annie's

lap this time. Why, this was a story she could write in her diary! And when she did, she would find the humor in the great chick chase.

"Go away," Annie said, pushing him off.

He tried Mary, imploring her to speak to him. She of all people knew what it was to be naughty!

She put her hands under her chin and frowned, refusing to pet him.

He had long observed that younger children were much quicker to forgive, so he tried his sweet Pearl next. Tate had his arms around her as she covered her eyes and moaned something about never being able to look at him again. This hurt his feelings excruciatingly, as sensitive Pearl had *never* been mad at him, had always given him the benefit of the doubt.

None of the children were the least bit friendly that morning except for Ezra, who gave him a half-hearted pat, and Sweetums, who did not seem to remember. He took solace in her squeezing and pulling at him before he trotted off, sniffing the ground until he was at the forsythia bush, where his bird treasure was buried. Since they were ignoring him, he hoped they wouldn't notice. But now even this gave him little comfort.

"What's he doing?" Pearl asked.

"That's where he buried it," Ezra said, bouncing his basketball on the driveway.

"By *it*, do you mean our dear, *sweet Lavinia*?" Annie said, standing up. She folded her arms and scowled at Lord Tennyson.

"Don't be mad at Tenny," Ezra said.

"I *am* mad at him!" Annie snapped, stomping back into the house.

"He didn't mean to," Tate said weakly.

"Of course he did! He's a dog, and dogs eat birds," Ezra said, swishing a two-point shot.

"But Lavinia was our *pet*," Pearl said, bursting into fresh tears.

"Not really," Ezra said. "I can't even tell the chickens apart. Are you sure it was even Lavinia?"

"Of course we're sure! And we should have a funeral for *Lavinia*," Mary said. "For . . . what's left of her." They all glanced uneasily at the forsythia bush.

"Ten Ten," Sweetums said, crawling down the front porch steps. She pointed at him accusingly. Great, now even the baby was angry with him and might never learn to walk.

"How will we have a funeral for Lavinia . . . without . . . Lavinia?" Pearl said.

"Dig her up?" Tate suggested, looking at the forsythia bush.

"Probably not much left," Ezra said.

Pearl wailed.

That wasn't exactly true, but Lord Tennyson had no intention of presenting the evidence. They wouldn't understand or appreciate the love he had for his precious bird.

"We'll have a memorial thervith inthtead," Tate said, patting Pearl. Lord Tennyson heard a sigh and looked up to see Annie moping on the window seat in her bedroom, hand under her chin. In her hands was the diary. His hopes rose and fell in an instant. Instead of writing about Naughty Mary . . . she would name *him* as the naughty one.

Mary emerged from the house with a shoebox, having missed the prior conversation.

"This," she said, showing her siblings, "can be her coffin."

"I'm *not* digging her up!" Pearl yelled.

"Ezzie!" Annie interrupted, yelling from the upstairs window. "Go get the baby!"

Sweetums had escaped their attention and was making her way across the front lawn. Except this time, she was not crawling but taking one wobbly step after another.

"She's walking!" Ezra said. "Sweetums is walking. Come see!"

"I refuse to be in the same vicinity as Lord Tennyson!" Annie yelled back. If she was trying to make him feel excluded and unwanted, she was doing a good job of it. How many times had he forgiven her? Forgiven all of them? Not long ago he'd been abandoned in the treehouse for hours!

He shook this off and took off after Sweetums, joyous that she was indeed walking, especially as he'd interrupted her first steps during the chicken chase. She happily shrieked when she saw him coming for her, first grabbing his ears, then his middle, and they rolled across the grass. Normally he did not like this game, but now he relished it. They lay on the grass with the summer sunshine on their faces until they heard a loud voice.

"Ahem."

He scrambled up and assumed the posture of a dignitary.

It was Mrs. Gage out walking Fat Cat on a diamond-encrusted leash, Widdy Boo and Nuff sauntering behind. Sweetums squealed, standing up and trying to take a wobbly step toward the fluffball. Fat Cat rudely did not acknowledge Sweetums. Instead, she walked away, her big bushy white tail high in the sky like she was the queen of the country. But then the other children chased after her. They began to pet and fawn over Fat Cat, who finally twisted onto her back so they could rub her belly. She looked at Lord Tennyson through her small slitted eyes, and a snobbish smile punctuated her satisfied purrs. Long tufts of her cat hair wafted into the air. Lord Tennyson sneezed and looked up at the sky as if he were most uninterested and not as deeply hurt as he felt.

Mrs. Gage sniffed in his direction instead of showering him with compliments as she usually did. Lord Tennyson would have liked to point out that Fat Cat had eaten many birds in her lifetime and *she* wasn't getting the silent treatment. Still, perhaps Mrs. Gage would set a good example of forgiveness for the children if he asked nicely. So when Mrs. Gage continued on her walk with Fat Cat, Lord Tennyson trotted behind them.

Mrs. Gage was not in a forgiving mood.

"No," she said loudly. "Stay! Stay!"

Fat Cat turned and hissed at Lord Tennyson. He stopped short just as she stuck out her big hairy paw and clawed him on the nose. It hurt terribly.

"Kitty!" Mrs. Gage said, too late. "Be nice."

Fat Cat hissed again and resumed her walk, pulling Mrs. Gage with her.

The children ran to him, their grudge instantly forgotten in his hour of need.

"Oh, Tenny!" Pearl cried. "He's bleeding."

"Come on, boy," Ezra said, picking him up.

"He needth a Band-Aid!" Tate hollered.

"Oh boy, poor boy," Mary said.

Lord Tennyson was angry about being scratched by the nasty feline, but he would have endured a hundred scratches to be back in the children's good graces.

"Is he okay?" Even Annie yelled from the window.

Ezra found a Band-Aid and put it on Lord Tennyson's nose. It pulled at his fur, but pawing at it only made Fat Cat's scratch feel worse.

Mary picked up the shoebox. "Come on," she said.

"You, too, Lord Tennyson. We must have a funeral and say sorry."

Except for Annie, who stubbornly stayed at her window, the children followed Mary out into the field, past Honey's garden beds and compost pile. Lord Tennyson went after them, carrying Sweetums through the grass when she became tired of her newfound toddling skills. He knew the spot well. He had accompanied the McNiffs to many funerals for frogs, a pet mouse, and countless fish.

"Ith Lavinia going to Puppy Planet?" Tate asked. "That'th where all the dogth go, right, Pearl?"

"We're burying a chicken," Ezra said. "Not a dog."

Mary grabbed a small shovel from the compost and made a hole in the ground. Lord Tennyson joined in the digging. (It was the least he could do.) Mary opened the shoebox. Even though he knew where his bird was, he peered inside the shoebox anyway. There was a single sheet of paper with writing and a yellow chick drawn on it and a yellow Magic Marker.

Pearl began to sniff.

"No more crying," Mary said. "She's in chick heaven, and our offering will bring her great solace in the afterworld."

"Ith it *like* Puppy Planet?" Tate asked, brightening.

Lord Tennyson was proud of Mary and the way she was comforting the children. And wasn't it a wonderful thought—a chick heaven! A place where there was nothing but birds! It sounded even more appealing than a Puppy Planet.

Mary began to read her note aloud:

"Dear Lavinia, Tenny ate you yesterday, and we are very sorry. I had a nightmare about it last night. Just remembering your flopping legs . . ."

Pearl shrieked and clung to Tate.

"Sorry," Mary said, and continued. "Dearest Lavinia, may you rest in peace under the forsythia bush. We loved you and will never forget you. Love, Mary and the McNifficents." Lord Tennyson smiled at the name. So did the children.

"The McNifficents!" Ezra said. "That's what we'll be from now on."

Pearl went next and drew a picture of a chick that looked like a circle with two legs. "I'm sorry I couldn't save you like I saved the bunnies," she said sadly. "I will try harder next time."

Tate wrote a note that looked like very heartfelt scribbles.

Ezra sighed and just signed his name.

Lord Tennyson stepped on the note, leaving a dirty paw print.

Sweetums drooled on the box before it was buried in the ground and covered with a large rock.

The children held hands, bonding over the Lavinia tragedy. For the first time since he had eaten the chicken, Lord Tennyson saw a positive. Along with the memory of Lavinia, perhaps they had also buried all their bad feelings for one another.

"Good-bye, Lavinia," Mary said. "We are sorry you came to a very bad end."

Annie, who being absent from the funeral had not buried her mean feelings, was unpleasant and short tempered when Mary and Lord Tennyson came into the bedroom later. She acted as if Mary were somehow to blame for what happened. Sadly, this was something he'd observed about humans. When they were gloomy and unhappy, they most often blamed the people they loved best.

This fight between them had gone on far longer than he'd expected. How would they get past their irritations and petty differences? Could siblings as unalike as Annie and Mary share a room and still be respectful to each other? He would like to consult an expert on the matter. If the librarian allowed him in the library, he would get his own library card and check out a book about it. Unfortunately, along with the beach, that was one of the only places in town he was not allowed.

"I hope that someday Annie can like me even a little bit," Mary said when Annie left the room. He comforted her by putting his head on her knee, hoping for the same thing. That night he fell asleep on their floor. And even though he had apologized publicly at the funeral and meant it, he dreamed of birds. Big, beautiful, unnamed birds that looked an awful lot like chickens.

CHAPTER FIFTEEN

Lord Tennyson Goes to the Library

IT WAS A SATURDAY MORNING IN LATE JULY, AND ANNIE had changed her outfit five times. Lord Tennyson had brought her the bright-striped shorts and blue top she had inherited from Christie Lundeen, because it was their shared favorite.

"Thank you, Tenny," she said, finally conceding her anger toward him. But she kept hesitating, taking both articles of clothing on and off.

Lord Tennyson guessed she was still smarting from Megan's comment about hand-me-downs. With so many kids, the McNiffs rarely bought anything new. The bag of clothes she had been gifted was thrilling, and Lord Tennyson wanted Annie to wear her new-to-her clothes with pride and not let anyone squash her soul. How to remind Annie that if Megan was a true friend, she would champion Annie, not make fun of her.

"I should just wear it, shouldn't I?" Annie said, seemingly coming to the conclusion all on her own.

Lord Tennyson nodded. She finally nodded at herself in the mirror, kissed him on the nose, and went downstairs to get picked up for the summer fair. He accompanied her to the car, barking good-bye and warning Megan to be nice.

"Good-bye!" Annie yelled. "I love you!" Lord Tennyson beamed, happy to be loved again, at least by the children.

Mr. McNiff and Honey were on the porch and waved good-bye to Annie. He was halfway up the front steps when he heard Mr. McNiff say they still needed to find a costume for his lead actor. Honey responded by saying they couldn't leave the children alone so soon after "the incident."

Alone? They were *never* alone! They had him at every waking—and unwaking—moment! As for "the incident," would they never forgive and forget the Lavinia debacle? Did one error in judgment truly erase all the good he had done? He was nearly disconsolate, even when his beloved Honey fed him the last bite of her bacon. Perhaps it was only a last treat before it was off to the senior dog home!

Once back inside, he became more attentive and insistent than usual, ensuring that each child completed their chore chart. (Annie had made an attempt before leaving, but Sweetums participated only by licking the broom and putting her toes in her cereal bowl.) Chores finally complete, Lord Tennyson felt a little better and allowed Mary and Ezra to skip outside to their bikes.

Together they pedaled away from the pink farmhouse on Marigold Lane into town with Lord Tennyson chaperoning. This time, instead of making him run the whole way, Mary had lifted him up into her basket.

He barked a *good morning* at the Goody farm in general, then at the water buffalo, Rembrandt, Ms. Monet, and Baby Munch.

"What a cushy life they have," Mary said. "They just

eat and wander and never have to do math or piano lessons or *chores*. I wish I could be that lazy." As soon as she said this, Rembrandt looked up.

"But you don't get to ride a bike, do you, old Rembrandt? Want to try?" Ezra asked.

Mary shrieked with laughter before saying, "I guess you're right. I wouldn't want to be a buffalo if I couldn't ride a bike." Rembrandt mooed and tossed his head in agreement. While Lord Tennyson still did not have his own bike, at least he got to ride in one. He had always felt sorry for other animals who did not have a special place in the McNiff family, who did not get to ride in baskets to town. He hoped his bike-riding-special-basket days weren't numbered.

"Wait up!" Ezra yelled.

Mary grinned but only picked up speed, pedaling furiously as they approached the downhill.

"Woo-wee!" Mary shrieked.

How fast Mary rode! How exhilarating to fly down a hill!

She hunched on the descent, her red flag up high and waving behind her, making that delicious wind-flapping sound. Ezra applied the brakes a little more judiciously until he too let go and was coasting down the hill, past the tall one-hundred-year-old trees on either side of the road.

Lord Tennyson panted with exhilaration, his long pink tongue flapping like the red flag, the wind blowing back his ears and long eyebrows.

Today, like almost every Saturday, they were meeting Lori at the library before going to Bellows Grocery, where Mary would surely buy a jar of pickles and a box of ice cream bars, spending every penny of her weekly allowance. Annie and Ezra were more likely to save their allowance for something special, but not Mary. She always spent it immediately, usually on treats.

Mary and Ezra found Lori by the library bike racks, her cowlick sticking right up in front, while the rest of her red hair was pulled back into a ponytail.

Together, Mary and Lori skipped up the library ramp, Mary's books jumping up and down in her backpack.

"Come on!" Mary called to Lord Tennyson.

He growled, about to curl up in the bike basket for a nap. After all, he wasn't allowed in the library, though that never seemed to matter to Mary.

"We could take turns going in," Ezra suggested.

"That's no fun, Ezra McNiff!"

She picked Lord Tennyson up and put him on the ground. "Be good," she warned, wagging her finger at him. The ridiculousness of this statement was not lost on him.

They entered the library in stealth mode, Mary pulling Lord Tennyson behind her. This was one of Mary's new favorite activities: sneaking Lord Tennyson into the library without getting caught by Ms. Melanie Moonie. Trespassing was one of Lord Tennyson's least favorite activities. (Though, truly, Mary McNiff would be much better behaved if he were to get an invitation to enter with her.)

Mary pressed herself against the wall and peeked around the corner. The librarian was sitting at her desk, humming while putting a clear cover on a book.

"Create a distraction," Mary said.

"You do it," Lori said. "You're better at it."

"Hello, young ladies," Ms. Melanie called without looking up from her book.

The girls giggled.

"Ladies!" Ezra wrinkled his nose, but he lit up when Mary looped her arm in his, happy to be included in Mary's gang.

Just as Mary was about to fake an allergic reaction to bees, Ms. Melanie turned her back and answered the telephone.

"Now!"

They were off, sprinting through the corridor, past the librarian's desk, and into the children's room. Lord Tennyson made it into the children's room, sniffing, undetected.

He would have liked to browse the child-minding section, but Mary tucked him under a chair and Ezra brought him a stack of Curious George books. He had to admit, he liked the monkey, even though he was very naughty. After reading and looking at the beautifully drawn pictures, he took a snooze on the soft carpet of colorful ABC letters, hidden from view from other children who wandered into the room.

When they had finally decided on their books to check out, Mary smiled her wicked smile.

"And now," she whispered, "it's time to pull the bell!"

"But then we can't check out our books," Ezra said.

"She won't know it's us," Mary said.

"Yes! You do it!" Lori said.

Lord Tennyson's ears perked up, and he gave her his

sternest look. Not the bell again! Why did Mary insist on testing the new librarian this way instead of becoming friends with her?

Hanging from the ceiling in the children's room was a long, thick rope that led to the town hall bell, which signaled important events. Ms. Melanie followed the tradition of previous librarians and did not allow children to ring the bell, though it was simply preposterous to put a long rope in a children's room and not expect every child to want to pull on it. Fortunately for the town, one had to climb up on the bookcase and pull the rope very, very hard for the bell to ring. Most children were simply not strong enough—nor daring enough.

But Mary McNiff was not most children.

"Or," Ezra said, "we could check out our books—which is why we came to the library—and walk out the door like normal people?" Lord Tennyson agreed, stepping toward the exit.

"Don't be a chicken!" Mary said.

Chicken! Lord Tennyson was trying not to think about chickens ever again.

Mary turned to Lori. "Keep a lookout. After I ring

the bell, when Ms. Melanie gets up from her chair, yell 'peanut butter!' and Tenny and I will escape through that door," Mary said, pointing to the door they usually entered through. "If for some reason she goes around through the back door, yell . . . 'jelly!'"

"I'll pull the bell," Ezra said, smarting from being called a chicken. "I'm stronger."

"No, it's my idea!"

"Fine, but if we get caught and thrown in jail, you remember that."

Lord Tennyson shook his head. His children in jail!

Mary climbed up onto the bookshelf and steadied herself. She grinned at them before saying, "Ready, Tenny?"

With parents browsing in other sections, the small toddlers and children reading books on the ABC rug looked delighted to discover that there was not only a dog in the library but a daredevil.

Lord Tennyson wanted to bark a *No, I am not ready, Naughty Mary!* But if he barked, that would surely bring Ms. Melanie running.

He could also tell by the look on Mary's face that she didn't care whether or not Lord Tennyson approved anyway. Just when he thought they were making progress with her behavior, here she was, readying herself to jump onto a rope.

Desperate to stop her, he climbed up and wrapped himself around her leg. Mary only laughed, as if she thought Lord Tennyson wanted to fly through the air with her. With Lord Tennyson wrapped around her leg, she reached out, grabbed the rope, and jumped from the shelf. He hung on for his life! The rope hardly moved as they swayed back and forth. Lord Tennyson gulped and tried not to look down. The toddlers cheered, but no bell sound rang out.

Emboldened, Mary said, "More weight! Ezra—jump on!"

Ezra hesitated, but under Mary's threatening glare he jumped and swung, finally making the bell ring, a long and glorious sound—at the very same moment Ms. Melanie came walking into the room, much earlier than expected.

Lori shrieked. She had been so enthralled watching the three of them that she had forgotten to keep watch. Still wound around Mary's leg, swinging through the air with two naughty McNiffs who did not yet see they'd been caught, Lord Tennyson had no choice but to bark, *Peanut butter!*

"Mary McNiff?" Ms. Melanie said. "EZRA!? AND— is that a DOG?!"

Mary, Ezra, and Lord Tennyson swung from the great rope in shock as it bobbed up and down. . . . *Ring, ring, ring . . .*

The babies cried and the toddlers went berserk, running around the room, laughing at the marvelous morning entertainment.

"Peanut butter, peanut butter, peanut butter!" Lori screamed, too late.

Ms. Melanie was momentarily distracted by the commotion.

"Where?" she yelled. "Where's the peanut butter?"

If there was anything more terrible than ringing a bell or a dog in the library—it was *food* in the library! Sticky, smudgy, staining-book-pages peanut butter!

She turned her head, which was fortuitous, meaning it worked highly in Mary and Ezra's favor. They jumped down from the rope and ran. Lord Tennyson miraculously managed to let go in time and land without injury on the soft carpet. Oh, how he would like to explain and apologize to Ms. Melanie! But this was not the time. Instead, he chased the children out of the room, into the adult section, weaving through the fiction and nonfiction, past the front desk, and out the front door.

"WHERE IS THE PEANUT BUTTER?" Ms. Melanie's voice echoed through the open windows. The children on the rug laughed and asked for a snack, which made Mary shriek with laughter.

Mary and Lori hopped on their bikes.

But the vigilant Lord Tennyson looked around.

For some reason, Ezra was not out of the library yet! Lord Tennyson instantly barked, *We forgot Ezra!*

Mary slowed and turned, looking desperately at Lord Tennyson. He stared at her, reminding her—*The strength of the McNiff family is their love for one another.*

Letting out a frustrated and exaggerated sigh, Mary pedaled back until she found a distraught Ezra hopping on his bike.

"She's calling our parents!"

Lori looked like she was going to burst into tears.

"Why the heck didn't you run? What's wrong with you?" Mary said.

"I . . . She caught me!"

Mary rolled her eyes.

"I'm sorry," Ezra said, sniffing. Lord Tennyson could tell he was worried he'd be excluded from future library Saturdays. "I'll buy you a treat at Bellows," he offered her.

Mary smiled. "Okay, now stop crying and pedal. That was so fun!"

Lord Tennyson harrumphed. This was the problem: Mary thought being naughty was fun. And even worse, Lori and Ezra looked at each other and instead of standing up to her, they were soon, once again, following the leader. Mary smiled at Lord Tennyson. "You're a good dog even though you barked."

He couldn't believe it—he had barked "peanut butter" *for* Mary, not against her.

They parked their bikes across the street from Bellows Grocery.

"Come on, Tenny," Mary said. "Remember, no barking this time, or mean old Baldy Bellows will cut you up into sausage."

Lord Tennyson hung his head.

"How about Tenny and I stay here?" Lori said, sitting under a tree and pulling him onto her lap. "Get the usual?"

"Of course!" Mary yelled. "Come on, Ezzie."

"Uh," Ezra said, patting his pockets. "My money's at home."

"Well, come on. You can pay me back."

Lord Tennyson, held back by Lori, watched as Ezra and Mary entered the store that he was actually allowed in, envious of the air-conditioning and cold linoleum floor. He also felt a foreboding he could not shake. Mary, emboldened by successfully ringing the bell, was in a very mischievous mood.

"Shut the door, McNiff!" he heard Mr. Bellows holler, even though the doors were automatic. "You're letting all the cold air out." Lord Tennyson saw Mary stick her tongue out behind Mr. Bellows's back while she and Ezra hustled away from him and his dingy white apron.

Lord Tennyson could picture where Mary was because she always used the same route on Saturday morning: first she touched all the produce without buying anything, then worked her way to the pickles and, last of all, the ice cream sandwiches.

"Do you want to be *my* pet dog?" Lori asked, giving him a drink from her water bottle as they waited. Lori was nice enough, but Lord Tennyson shook his head politely. Even though there was only one Lori and six McNiffs, they were his charges for life.

Finally, he saw Ezra and Mary through the big window, standing at the cash register. Mary was holding the pickles and ice cream bars. She put them down in front of the cashier and dug through her pockets, front and back. Something was wrong—she didn't have her money either!

Even with his superior hearing, Lord Tennyson could not hear what the cashier was saying, but he gathered that whatever Mary was asking for, she was not getting. He nudged Lori with his nose, but Lori lay on her back, looking at clouds.

The cashier grabbed her microphone, and Lord Tennyson's ears perked up. "Mr. Bellows," the cashier said. "To the front, please, Mr. Bellows."

Mary began waving her hands *no*, but he could see Mr. Bellows already thundering down the aisle toward the cash register. He was so sweaty, the ceiling lights reflected off his bald head.

Ezra melted behind Mary, who looked like she wanted to disappear into the shiny linoleum floor herself.

Mr. Bellows put his hands on his hips and said something that made Ezra look like he was about to cry again. Lord Tennyson knew Mary would not cry. Her jaw clenched shut as she glared at Mr. Bellows and took the pickles and ice cream sandwiches off the conveyor belt.

Lord Tennyson pawed at the ground and whined, but Lori did not move. Not knowing what to do, but wanting to do something, Lord Tennyson broke free from Lori's grasp and raced across the street. He dodged a yellow car and an orange bike, leaped over the curb, and ran to the window.

"Come back!" Lori yelled.

Mr. Bellows stomped back down the aisle as Lord Tennyson ran into the store, the door automatically opening for him. He stood next to Mary as she looked from the cold pickles to the ice cream.

"Mary . . . ?" Ezra said.

Mary . . . Lord Tennyson poked her on the leg with his paw.

Because Mary had *that look* on her face.

"Take it and go," she whispered to Ezra, putting the food in his hands.

Ezra shoved it back at her. "No!"

"Well, just GO!" she hissed.

And then, while the cashier wasn't looking, Mary raised her chin and, still holding the pickles and ice cream bars, walked toward the front doors until she was all the way through them.

Without paying.

An alarm did not sound. The cashier didn't come running after them. Baldy didn't arrest them.

What Mary didn't see, but Lord Tennyson did, was Cal Hubbard, staring after them, a strange look on his face. *You see*, Lord Tennyson wanted to say to Mary, *nothing naughty you do is ever really a secret.*

Lord Tennyson ran after Mary.

"Mary!" Ezra whispered after her. "Put it back!"

Mary crossed the street and shoved the food into her backpack without a word.

Whistling, she got on her bike, but not before throwing a bone at Lord Tennyson that he had not seen her carrying. Had she stolen that, too? "Even got my best pal a bone!" she crowed.

"I thought *I* was your best pal," Lori said.

"After Tenny, of course," Mary said.

Lord Tennyson felt too sick to even pick up his bone. He left it there on the sidewalk and ran after the two girls as they pedaled down the street.

Ezra caught up, out of breath.

"Mary, go back!"

"It's your fault. You said you were going to buy me a treat, and my hopes were up so high."

"I told you I didn't have any money!"

"Well, I lost my money and couldn't go back to find it because *you* got caught!"

Ezra's face crumpled.

Mary's face smoothed into complete innocence. "Let's eat the ice cream first, before it melts." Coming across a small pavilion, she laid her bike on the ground and hid behind a tree.

Together, Mary and Lori shoved ice cream sandwiches into their mouths at warp speed, not slowing to lick, nibble, or discuss the latest family and school gossip as they usually did. Ezra and Lord Tennyson refused all offers of food.

They stared at her without a word.

"What's wrong?" Lori said, pausing midbite to look at them.

"Nothing," Mary said. She gulped, suppressing the secret with another bite.

Lord Tennyson was not impressed. He was appalled, saddened, and distressed.

"Be quiet, Tenny," Mary commanded. She knew full well he hadn't said a word, but his disapproving glare was effective.

Next was the pickles. The entire jar.

"Hiding the evidence," Ezra muttered, staring at Mary.

Mary, looking a little greenish, tried to grin anyway.

"I'm feeling . . ." A loud burp escaped her mouth, and the smell of pickles wafted through the air.

Just then a shadow appeared over the girls, scaring them so badly they screamed. Lord Tennyson, on full alert, began barking.

"Whoa, whoa," the shadow said.

Mary jumped up. "Cal?"

"Hi, Cal," Ezra said nervously.

"You're in on this too?" he asked.

Ezra's face drained of color.

Mary burped again, clapping her hand over her mouth.

"What do you want?" Lori asked.

"I, uh, work at Baldy's, you know," Cal began.

Mary nodded.

"I . . . saw what you did."

Ezra's eyes widened.

Lori looked from Cal to Mary.

They stared at each other for an agonizing five seconds until Mary broke the staring contest by doing the next least honorable thing: she ran.

Lord Tennyson barked for her to return, but Mary hopped on her bike and began to pedal.

"Bye!" Lori hopped on her own bike, pedaling off in the opposite direction.

"I'll . . . I'll make it right!" Ezra yelled to Cal.

Lord Tennyson and Ezra chased after Mary, who pedaled furiously until the town was behind her, the buildings smaller and smaller. But Mary couldn't outride what she had done. No, it never worked like that. Her pedaling became slower and slower. Twice she leaned over her handlebars as if she were about to be sick.

They made it to the pink house just before Mary rolled off her bike and stumbled to the forsythia bush. There she hurled up seven pickles and four ice cream sandwiches,

Lord Tennyson by her side. Also witnessing was a small, coiled garter that looked remarkably like Ezra's snake. He let it slither away unnoticed.

"I think I'm going to die," Mary moaned, holding her stomach. When she finally looked over at him, he refused to look the least bit sympathetic.

Ezra couldn't either. He threw his bike onto the yard, shook his head at Mary, and went into the house. They both could hear Ezra stomp upstairs and slam his bedroom door shut.

Mary flopped on the ground and burst into tears.

CHAPTER SIXTEEN

A Great Guilt

AN HOUR LATER MARY LAY IN BED, THE COVERS pulled high over her head. Lord Tennyson lay on the floor like a dog does in times of distress. Honey had clucked and sequestered Mary from the rest of the family because if there was anything worse than having one child down with the stomach bug, it was having *six* down.

Ezra had looked so forlorn that Honey had put her hand on his forehead and asked if he too was sick. He had silently shaken his head. Lord Tennyson knew that it was the shake of devastating disappointment not just in his hero, but also in himself for not stopping her.

As her caretaker (and now a long-distance sprinter), Lord Tennyson took Mary's thievery so personally that he too was ill. How could she have done such a wicked thing, *his* Mary? She had done horrid things before, like tattling and pulling hair when her temper got the best of her. She was mischievous, reading secret diaries, sneaking him into the library, and pulling pranks like spray-painting old fences with forbidden love poems. But *stealing*? Lord Tennyson felt a sharp tightness within his chest. His despair was almost too great to bear. He had hoped that with age, Mary's naughtiness would mellow, that her spunky, self-assertive drive would make her a leader, not put her on the cover of a Most Wanted poster. He had thought they were making progress together.

Mary moaned with stomach pains while Lord Tennyson moaned along with her. He hoped that she was having a reckoning with not just her gluttony but her conscience, because he was suddenly forced to reckon with *his*.

Days earlier, had he not stolen something that was not

exactly his to eat? He remembered the feeling of *having* to chase and eat Lavinia. What was that expression? Chickens coming home to roost. Meaning the past always catches up to us. Oh, the irony of *chickens*. Even now he almost couldn't help his mouth watering at the very thought.

Was he more like Mary than he cared to admit? Or worse, had she followed his example? Had his impulsive, unthinking act contributed to Mary's thievery?

Wretched thoughts spun webs in his head. Maybe Mr. McNiff and Honey were onto something. Maybe the children *did* need more. Someone who could either keep Mary in line or lock her in a tower. Someone who could help her choose what was right instead of . . . oh, such treachery!

He hadn't done enough to stop her and hadn't taught Ezra well enough to stand up to a future felon.

The summer of civilization was now well and truly torn to shreds. His dreams were shattered.

When Mary finally sat up and looked at him, she tried to keep a defiant look on her face.

"Say something," she said. "Tell me you're disappointed. I know you are."

He lay on the floor, momentarily incapable of expression.

When he stayed silent, her facade crumbled and she rolled around in her bed, the sheets getting entangled around her legs.

"He saw me, Tenny. Cal *saw* me! He's going to tell Baldy, and Baldy will tell Mom and Dad, and oh . . . I'm as good as dead!"

Lord Tennyson frowned. He had hoped Mary would feel bad for her lack of integrity, not because she had gotten caught.

When Mary stuck one hand out from under her comforter, reaching for him, he was so bereft of happiness that he couldn't even rise to lick her fingers for pickle juice and ice cream. Under different circumstances he would have enjoyed it.

Mary peeked out from her covers.

"Who cares!" she said, mustering up renewed defiance. "Who cares if I took them. Baldy Bellows is a mean stink bug who deserved it." She frowned. "Stop looking at me like that, Tenny. I don't care, and you can't make me care."

She pulled the comforter over her head again.

There was a very long silence.

The two of them lay still.

"I'm sorry, Tenny. I really am," came her muffled voice, finally. "It's just that—I was so embarrassed I lost my money, and I could just imagine what Annie would say!"

Lord Tennyson's ears perked up.

"I won't do it again, okay?" she finally whispered. "On my sacred honor."

Well, it was a start. But perhaps a start for someone else, because at that moment, he truly felt his chances of reforming the McNiffs . . . were over.

At dinnertime Honey brought a small bowl of broth and a slice of bread.

"It's from Osbert," she said.

Lord Tennyson sniffed it suspiciously, then took a nibble. It was slightly sour but surprisingly delicious. Mary looked at it and held her stomach. "Anything but pickles and ice cream sandwiches."

The floor creaked outside the bedroom.

Lord Tennyson recognized the familiar footsteps.

"Mary?" came Pearl's and Tate's voices.

Mary lay back down.

"Mary, Mary, Mary, are you alive?"

She pulled down the covers, and baby Sweetums crawled on top of Lord Tennyson's back while Tate and Pearl stood sweetly before her.

"We made you cards," Pearl said, bringing watercolor paintings out from behind her back.

Sweetums's drawings were scribbles, and Pearl and Tate had done their best with their letters and spelling, writing *I Luv U*.

Ezra slowly walked into the room as Annie peeked her head in the bedroom door. "Is she puking?" Annie asked.

"No," Ezra said.

"Faking?"

Mary scowled.

"What'th wrong, Mary?" Tate asked.

"Cal was looking for you today," Annie said, still standing in the doorway.

Mary turned a whiter shade of pale.

"What did you do this time?" Annie asked.

Mary turned her head.

"I'm calling a Sibling Council," Ezra said. "So, Annie, you have to come in."

Annie raised her eyebrows, but she took exactly one step forward. Huddled on the bed, Tate and Pearl turned on their flashlights because flashlights were always more fun than overhead lights. The McNiffs all turned to look at Annie.

But it was Ezra who spoke up.

"Stop acting like idiots," he said.

"Bad word," Tate whispered.

"What do you mean?" Annie asked. "Who's acting like an idiot?"

"You both are," Ezra said. "We want to have a good summer, but you're both always fighting and nobody likes it. You think it's all about you, but it's not. It makes everyone sad and puts all of us in the middle, which isn't fair."

"She stole my diary and painted words on the fence!" Annie said.

"But you made fun of her bed-wetting in front of everyone," argued Ezra.

"Exactly! She's mean!" Mary burst out.

"But wasn't what you did just as mean?" Ezra said back. "And also . . . McNiffs don't steal," he went on, getting to the most pressing issue without calling Mary out in

236

front of her siblings. Lord Tennyson liked where this was going. "The punishment for stealing is a guilty conscience. Brothers and sisters are supposed to be good examples to each other. That's what Tenny would say."

Lord Tennyson wiped a tear from his eye.

"I'm sorry!" Mary burst out. "I'm sorry for everything! Do you *all* hate me now?"

Even though they thought she might be contagious, every McNiff gave Mary a hug. Except for Annie, who couldn't make herself get close enough to what she was convinced was a potentially deadly virus. But she did squeeze Mary's big toe somewhat affectionately. Then Lord Tennyson and Sweetums both gave Mary a very loving lick.

Perhaps Lord Tennyson had done a thing or two right after all.

CHAPTER SEVENTEEN

Saving Curtis Cornell

DAYS PASSED. HOT JULY AFTERNOONS TURNED INTO humid and scorching August ones. Since Ezra's intervention, the sisters were, if not kind, at least tolerable. Mary and Lori still went to the library on their bikes (and had a good heart-to-heart with Ms. Melanie) but were taking a break from the grocery store, pickles, and ice cream sandwiches. Mary was avoiding Bellows Grocery and Cal altogether and had still not worked up the courage to confess her crime to Baldy. It ate at Lord Tennyson. It ate at Ezra, too, who refused to go with them until she did. With every passing day, they only felt worse. Making things right was the only way Mary would be able to live with herself, but so far, despite her family apology, she refused to speak of it.

Sometimes the entire McNiff family went to the library together, as was the case this Saturday morning. This time, Lord Tennyson stayed outside. He tried to stay cool by lying under a pine tree but soon gave up trying to nap.

Naturally, all the library customers (except for Mrs. Snoot) stopped to pet him, especially the children. He tolerated them by sniffing their pants and shoes and pockets, hoping for crumbs of food. Lord Tennyson was so popular that more children checked out books when he was there just so they could come outside to read to him, and this pleased Ms. Melanie and her summer reading initiative immensely.

There was one boy, though, whom he still could not abide: Curtis Cornell.

Fortunately, Curtis had been away most of the summer,

and Lord Tennyson had not seen him since that memorable first summer day at the lake.

Unfortunately, August had brought him back in full force. Adding to Lord Tennyson's misfortune, Honey had put a leash on Lord Tennyson and tied him to a tree. She so rarely put a leash on him that Lord Tennyson despaired in its implications. At this rate, he hoped that when the new nanny arrived, he would at least be allowed to stay. It also meant that when the barbarian of a child arrived on the scene, he was helpless to run or hide. He heard Curtis Cornell's pointy cowboy boots crunch on the pine needles before he heard his voice.

"Doggeeeeeeeey!" The child-beast was on him immediately.

"Doggy, doggy, doggy!" Curtis giggled, pulling Lord Tennyson's ear. "I got you, doggy!"

"That's right, Curtis," his dad said. "That's a doggy. Pearl and Tate's doggy. Maybe they're inside; should we go see?"

Ugh. There was that undignified word again: "doggy."

"No!" Curtis shouted. "I want a doggy!"

"Come on now." Curtis's dad appeared perpetually bewildered and worn down, the type of parent who had forgotten that he was the one who was supposed to be in charge, not the other way around. Lord Tennyson always wished he could write him a training manual. *Courage, dear father!* is how he would start.

"No," Curtis whined. "I don't want to read stupid books. I want a dog."

Lord Tennyson felt very sorry for any dog who ended up with Curtis. Today he was wearing a long cape and a pirate hat like a miniature Captain Hook. Lord Tennyson eyed the long sharp stick he held.

It soon got worse. The smaller Cornell children watched their older brother poke Lord Tennyson and learned from their evil elder.

"I'm going inside, kids. Do you want to stay out here and pet the doggy?" *Honestly!*

Lord Tennyson managed to sit upright and shake Curtis off. He gave Curtis's father a very hard look, but he seemed oblivious to his son's threat to Lord Tennyson's mortality.

He opened the library door and proceeded to enunciate very slowly and loudly as if that might make Curtis have a change of heart. "OKAY, HONEY. I'LL BE INSIDE.

COME IN SOON, AND WE'LL READ BOOKS TOGETHER."

Curtis ignored his dad and continued terrorizing Lord Tennyson.

The smaller Cornells quickly grew bored and entered the library. Shortly after, Lord Tennyson could hear them yelling and throwing books off library bookshelves.

But Curtis did not tire of playing the dance-and-dodge game with Lord Tennyson's life. At least as he moved around, Lord Tennyson had an occasional view of Pearl and Tate in the children's room. They were reading *Madeline*, a McNiff favorite. He had spent countless hours practicing their read-aloud chapter books with the McNiffs and had once hoped to be invited as a substitute teacher at the children's school. Ever since Pearl's teapot adventure, she had liked the story of the brave little French girl who was not afraid of anything. His pride swelled to see them having finally caught the reading bug. After reaching the last page, Pearl looked up and saw Mr. Cornell and the little Cornells but no Curtis. She grabbed Tate's hand and rushed to the window. Curtis was still slowly circling Lord Tennyson with his long stick. Well, if he was to perish, he was glad for a witness.

"Oh no!" Pearl's voice wafted through the cracked window.

"It'th that very bad boy," Tate said.

Pearl, using all her muscles, pushed at the window, trying to open it farther.

Tate joined her, and together they pushed until the window opened almost twelve inches.

"Hey, you!" Tate yelled.

"Stop it, you boy!" Pearl shouted to Curtis.

But Curtis Cornell only laughed maniacally and leaped onto Lord Tennyson's back. He jumped up and down, holding on to Lord Tennyson's fur like a bull rider.

"Yeehaw!" he yelled, giving Lord Tennyson a big kick in the ribs. "Ride 'em, cowboy."

Lord Tennyson yelped and bolted forward, but the leash held him tight. The movement was at least enough to knock Curtis off his back. Lord Tennyson quickly unwound himself exactly two times.

"My dog! My dog!" Tate yelled. "That bad boy ith hurting my Tenny!"

"Tenny?" It was Honey's voice!

"Ow!" Curtis wailed. "You hurt me, doggy!" He rubbed

his head and looked around for his dad. Not seeing him, he stopped crying, stood up, and ran toward Lord Tennyson, who dodged and darted to the left. Curtis fell on the ground.

"Attaboy!" Tate said.

"Tenny . . . ," Pearl wailed, her hands squishing her cheeks.

Honey came to the window to see Curtis Cornell chasing Lord Tennyson around the pine tree, lunging and tackling whenever the leash became too short. Lord Tennyson had some advantage, as he was much quicker than Curtis Cornell and his leash was long enough for him to dart one way and then another, but then Curtis stepped on the leash and yanked Lord Tennyson to the ground by his neck.

"I got you, little doggy!"

Sweetums pulled herself up and let out a mighty shriek before biting down on the windowsill with her two front teeth.

"Let's go!" he heard Honey say.

Lord Tennyson saw Pearl and Tate rush from the window. He knew they would have to run out of the children's room, through the adult books, past Ms. Melanie's desk, and to the library door, where they would have to pull open a large iron handle. Would they make it in time?

Lord Tennyson heard his children's efforts to reach him from underneath the wretched Curtis. He could hear yells and screams even as he felt himself slowly getting crushed under Curtis's weight. Ribs, lungs, and heart began squeezing together.

Hardly breathing, he knew he must act, and act now!

He did something he only did under the most dire circumstances—he nipped Curtis right on his fleshy thigh.

Curtis Cornell wailed and rolled over twice, flipping Lord Tennyson over with him but, thankfully, letting go of his neck. Lord Tennyson jumped up as quickly as his joints allowed and stepped back defensively.

"You bit me! Ow, ow, ow! You bit me!" Curtis screeched. His eyes narrowed into vengeful slits.

Curtis lunged. Then something happened here that is called serendipity. That means something better than expected, almost as if by magic. Lord Tennyson's leash suddenly came untied from the tree. The handle lay on the ground, forming a small lasso. When Curtis Cornell stepped toward Lord Tennyson, the toe of his very pointy cowboy boot was caught in the lasso. Seeing his opportunity, Lord Tennyson ran to the right and pulled upward. The force lifted the boy up into the air as if he were flying.

"Aahhhh!" Curtis shouted, looking down from the tree branch from where he now hung upside down. "Aahhhh!"

Just then the McNiff family finally came running out of the library, followed by the Cornells.

"Curtis!" Mr. Cornell yelled. "What are you doing up in that tree?"

"The doggy did it to me," Curtis yelled. "The doggy did it."

They all turned to look at Lord Tennyson, who was quietly lying under the pine tree, trying to catch his breath.

"Don't tell me stories, Curtis Cornell!" his father yelled. "You got up there. Now you get down!"

Ezra picked up Lord Tennyson and rubbed his head.

"Poor buddy," he said. Lord Tennyson almost purred with relief.

By this time a crowd of library patrons had gathered underneath Curtis Cornell, who so enjoyed being the center of attention that he wailed louder and louder, attracting even more of it.

People from Main Street, hearing Curtis's loud wailing, started to gather too.

"Call 911!" someone yelled.

"We need a ladder," Honey suggested.

"Ask Bellows!"

"Anyone but Baldy!" Mary whispered.

Minutes later, though, Cal and Mr. Bellows did show up and leaned a very tall ladder against the tree. Mr. Bellows's face was bright red, and he was dripping with perspiration. He looked up at the tall ladder.

"A bit afraid of heights," Mr. Bellows confessed, scratching his bald head.

"I . . . should save him," Pearl whispered to Tate, clutching her Madeline book. "I can climb up high, remember?"

Lord Tennyson was so proud of how brave she was becoming. But this? This was too high!

"No," Tate said. "It'th my turn to be brave. I have to get the bad boy."

"Oh no you don't," Ezra said. "You are *not* going up that ladder."

"I'll come," Pearl whispered.

Tate patted Pearl's arm. "Thtay. Thumtimeth we can't

go together." And he scampered up the ladder before any-one could stop him. Lord Tennyson wanted to cover his eyes with his paw but could not look away.

"Tate!" Ezra yelled.

Mary made a move to follow him, but when she put her foot on the bottom rung, the ladder shifted. She stepped down and instead held on to steady it, a look of fright on her face.

"Oh my goodness," Honey said.

Lord Tennyson barked anxiously.

"Daddy!" Curtis shouted. By now, surely all the blood in his body was in his head.

"It's so high," Mary said, a slight quaver in her voice.

"Don't look down," Tate said to himself, speaking from his previous coaching experience with Pearl. His voice only shook a little.

"Wahhhhh!" Curtis Cornell wailed.

The ladder made strange groaning sounds.

The crowd shouted.

Tate broke his own rule and peeked. He saw his brother and sisters and their frightened faces.

Then his eyes found Lord Tennyson, who was suddenly

perfectly calm in the midst of the storm of people around him. Underneath his white eyebrows, his dark brown eyes found Tate's.

Trust yourself.

You are capable.

Save the boy.

Yes, even though Curtis was mean, they must help him.

Tate turned and looked back up at Curtis.

Because of his superior hearing, Lord Tennyson heard exactly what transpired.

"Come on," Tate said. "I'll help you get down."

"The doggy did it," Curtis blubbered. "Bad, mean doggy!"

"We *could* leave him here," Mary suggested from down below.

"No," Curtis begged. "Don't leave me here."

"All right," Tate said. "But you mutht promith, on your thacred honor, to never *ever* touch Lord Tennython again. Deal?"

Curtis nodded at the same time he wailed another "Waaah!"

Tate pulled Curtis's cape free and helped him clamber

upright onto the branch, then put his two feet on the ladder.

"Don't look down," Tate said. "Look up. Alwayth up."

As the two made it down safely, Pearl, still holding her Madeline book, could not help but whisper, "Serves you right, you little warthog, for what you did to our poor dog."

CHAPTER EIGHTEEN

The Stuff of Which Heroes Are Made

ANOTHER SUMMER SATURDAY ARRIVED.

Annie had gone off with friends to Bellows Grocery for s'mores ingredients—and to see Cal, who was working, but who thankfully had never caught on that the poem was about him. Making an effort to be more amiable toward her sister, Annie had even invited Mary to come along. Rarely invited to go anywhere with Annie, Mary was mourning having to decline and worrying what Cal might tell Annie.

"I wanted to go, Tenny," Mary said, lying on the floor of her bedroom with him. "But . . ."

Lord Tennyson licked her arm pointedly.

"If I confess, he'll yell really loud. What if he calls the police or murders me? What if he calls Mom and Dad?"

Lord Tennyson was also scared of these scenarios and how they would reflect on his child-minding abilities. But he was also more resigned, knowing children must face the consequences of their own choices, as he must. He could only hope that his influence had made a small difference and that Honey and Mr. McNiff might again see that in time.

"But you know how Baldy brought over that ladder for Curtis?" Mary mused. "That was pretty nice."

Lord Tennyson brightened! This was true. Perhaps Mr. Bellows had a heart after all.

"Ezra keeps saying I have to or I'll never be able to live with myself."

She sat up and tried to talk herself out of it.

"But does Baldy deserve a confession? He knew I was good for the money but still wouldn't let me take my snacks. He's never been nice to *me*."

Lord Tennyson frowned, stood, and pushed Mary toward Ezra's room before she could talk herself out of it further. He was sorry to wake his oldest boy. Ezra loved everything about summer vacation, but it was the sleeping-in part that was best of all. He looked like he was having a very good dream when Mary pounced on him.

Ezra, used to being pounced on, concentrated on not opening his eyes.

"Ezra," Mary whispered. "Wake up."

"Shhh. I'm about to make the winning shot."

"Ezra," Mary whispered again. She leaned forward, her eyes mere inches away from his, but he still refused to open them.

"What do you want?"

Mary clapped a hand over his mouth.

Ezra squirmed under the covers, but Mary had pinned him under the blankets so he couldn't use his arms or hands to pinch her.

"Sleeping!" he crossly said into her hand, but he finally opened his eyes.

Mary released her hold on his mouth.

Ezra stilled and immediately clamped his eyes shut again.

"Ezra," Mary said, sniffling. "I'm sorry I blamed you for stealing."

He opened one eye.

"I need your help."

Ezra opened the other eye.

That afternoon, after much procrastinating, Ezra and Mary rode their bikes back into town, once again chaperoned by Lord Tennyson in the bike basket. He was still not entirely sure what Mary would do. Confess and pay Bellows back, or end up repeating her thievery? Ezra had suggested Mary get a loan from Annie, but she had flatly refused, saying she would rather eat cold spaghetti off Baldy's head than confess to Annie.

To supplement Mary's lack of funds, Ezra emptied his piggy bank of pennies, nickels, dimes, and quarters. In addition, Mary now owed him five more personal favors on top of the five she had already granted him after he was her spray-painting accomplice.

Lord Tennyson had to admit he was impressed that Mary was walking back into Baldy Bellows's grocery store at all. But would she really do the right thing or lose her nerve?

They parked their bikes and stood together, staring at the Bellows Grocery sign.

"Go," Ezra said.

Mary gulped. "I'm going. But I can't talk to Baldy. Maybe Cal."

She entered the store, which was bustling with customers. She looked back one last time to make eye contact with Lord Tennyson, who stood silent and firm. Mary inhaled and took another step forward like an exiled queen to a guillotine.

She walked down every aisle in search of Cal, but he was busy working in the back.

Every once in a while, through the front store windows, Lord Tennyson could see Mr. Bellows stomping, looking grumpy as he swiped sweat from his shiny head with his old white apron.

Mary saw him several times too but did not approach. Even Ezra, safely outside, looked terrified. Mary turned to the cashier, laid down her money, and began to talk.

The cashier nodded, then put her mouth to the microphone.

"Mr. Bellows to the front, please, Mr. Bellows."

Ezra opened his mouth, but no sound came out.

Mary was shaking her head just like last time, *no, no, no!*

Lord Tennyson saw the panicked look in her eyes, the way she looked at the front door.

It was Lord Tennyson who ran this time, but not away. Instead, he stood in front of the automatic supermarket doors until they opened.

Mary took a step toward him. He raised a paw like they sometimes did to him. *Stop. Stay.*

He didn't enter the store, only stood in the doorway. He didn't trot forward or scratch the glass or bark. Instead, he summoned every bit of courage he could and sent it to her.

The doors stayed open and he watched Mary, his goatee and long white eyebrows wise and unflinching.

"Tenny," Mary mouthed. He wished he could go to her, protect her, but no, Mary must do this alone.

Baldy Bellows came down the aisle. His voice was loud as he bellowed behind him at the butcher to make smaller slices.

A baby cried.

A mother shushed.

"You can do it," Ezra whispered, having joined Lord Tennyson at the door.

Mary's eyes welled.

"What!" Mr. Bellows demanded.

She turned to face him.

"I, uh . . ."

Mr. Bellows looked at the cashier, exasperated.

The cashier shrank under his glare.

"Mr. Bellows," Mary began, her voice like a little mouse.

"What!" he bellowed again.

"Mr. Bellows, I'm here because—"

"No fundraisers," he interrupted.

"Wha . . . ?"

"I'm a very busy man, and I don't have the time to buy a chocolate Easter bunny or anything like that. This is my store. You want me to buy a chocolate bunny, you come to my house."

"No," Mary said. "I'm here because . . . I took . . . some pickles and ice cream sandwiches without paying and I'm very sorry and I came to repay you." Mary's face burned

red as she pushed the pennies and nickels and dimes forward.

"You *what*?" Mr. Bellows was no longer loud. His voice
was dangerously soft. "You *stole* from me?"

Mary nodded.

There was a terrible silence.

"You could go to jail for shoplifting." Bellows's face
darkened.

Ezra audibly gulped.

Mary hung her head.

Lord Tennyson was always proud of his children, but
there were times when he was especially so. This was one
of those times.

Bellows stared at the money.

"I'm sorry," Mary said again.

There was another long silence until he spoke.

"You knew I'd be angry," he said.

"Yes."

"You came anyway."

"Yes."

"Well," Mr. Bellows said. "I trust this will never occur
again."

"No. No, sir."

"Then get. And take your little dog, too." But this time he almost sounded kind.

Mary ran out of the store, hopped on her bike, and pedaled as fast as she could toward home. She did not try to find Annie or Lori or enter the library to browse for books or ring a bell she shouldn't.

Lord Tennyson ran, and when she slowed, he took the lead.

Eventually, Mary got off her bike and began walking. Ezra hopped off his and slung an arm over Mary's shoulders as she cried.

Lord Tennyson felt something shift in the universe.

The hope he had not dared to hope began to bloom again.

Perhaps not *all* was lost after all.

CHAPTER NINETEEN

Water Buffalo on the Loose!

"I'M NOT WATCHING IT!" ANNIE SAID.

"It's Sweetums's turn, so she gets to pick," Mary said, holding up the movie *All Dogs Go to Heaven*. Sweetums squealed.

Lord Tennyson paused at the movie choice. He enjoyed the great dog classics, except for the endings. They always made the McNiffs weep.

"Mine!" Sweetums said, grabbing the movie and

banging it on the floor. The bunnies, Felicity and Delilah, hopped out of the room and away from Sweetums.

That evening, their parents were out to dinner and had entrusted the children to Lord Tennyson's care. It was only a short absence, but no one else, including Mrs. Gage, had been asked to help mind the children. Lord Tennyson's heart had leaped at this second chance, and he wanted—no, *needed*—an exceptionally good outcome this evening.

They were off to a good start as, with his nudging, the children had eaten and somewhat cleaned up after themselves. Now, before bed, they were attempting to pick a movie to watch together. Lord Tennyson pondered how to best teach the art of negotiation; the McNiff children's skills were rather abysmal. Every suggestion was met with an aggressive objection.

"No dog movies," Annie said. She was wearing her English nightgown and thus was speaking once more as if she were queen. "I shan't cry tonight!"

"Puppy Planet," Tate said sadly.

Ezra sighed and threw himself onto the floor next to Lord Tennyson, who lay on his dog bed. This could go on all night. Sweetums took two steps and lay on top of him, sucking her thumb and twirling the sprouting hair atop her head.

"Remember *My Dog Skip*?" Annie said, quoting the last line in a dramatic drawl: "'He wasn't really gone . . . for he really lay buried in my heart.' Dogs shouldn't die— EVER!"

"No one died in *The Fox and the Hound*," Mary said.

"Ugh! It's just as bad," Annie said. "Todd and Copper grow up and can't ever be friends again."

Lord Tennyson sniffed.

Pearl and Tate began to sniff too.

"I don't want . . . our Tenny to ever go away," Tate hiccupped.

"Charlotte died," Pearl said, her eyes filling with tears.

"That was a spider, not a dog," Annie said.

"Bambi," Tate said, his lips quivering.

"E.T.," Pearl said.

"Oh geez," Ezra said, putting his arm around Tenny. "Can we please just watch a movie where *no* animals die?" He sat up. "Tate and I should pick since the girls always get to."

"How about *Creatureth from Outer Thpathe*?" Tate said.

"Or how about the zombie one?" Ezra said.

Lord Tennyson shook his head.

"Nicholas says no too," Pearl said, holding him up.

"Nicholas does *not* get a vote," Ezra said.

Lord Tennyson wondered when Osbert would start voting.

"Buth Lightyear!" Tate yelled, standing up on the couch. He put out his hands like Superman and flew off the couch, landing in a ball next to Lord Tennyson.

Sweetums laughed and kicked her feet, forgetting entirely that it had been her turn to pick.

Saving them from a night of endless debating, there was a knock on the door.

The children stopped talking and listened carefully.

"It's probably Mrs. Gage," Mary whispered. "Maybe she's checking on us again."

Lord Tennyson rose in a protective, but resigned, stance.

Ezra scrambled to hide behind the front door like a spy. "Don't let her in, or our fun is over."

The knocking came again, harder and more insistent.

Lord Tennyson crept forward and peeked through the curtain.

Sweetums crawled after him so fast that she thumped headfirst into the front door.

"Well, Mrs. Gage knows we're in here now," Annie said.

But it was not Mrs. Gage standing on the porch.

It was Mr. Goody.

Lord Tennyson gave a short bark to open the door.

Ezra did.

Mr. Goody was clearly in a panic.

He paced the porch, holding his gray cap and wringing the brim so hard his hands were turning the same shade of white as his face.

"Hey there, Mr. Goody," Ezra said.

"Are your, uh, parents home?" He peered in anxiously.

"Are you okay?" Ezra asked. By this time all the children were gathered at the door. Lord Tennyson still stood protectively in front of them.

"Our parents aren't here," Annie said tentatively. They weren't ever supposed to tell anyone that, but there was something about Mr. Goody's face.

"Have you, uh, by any chance seen Ms. Monet? Or Rembrandt?"

"The water buffalo?" Tate asked, squeezing his head in between Ezra's legs to get a better look.

"Yes. They got out."

The children shook their heads. All except Pearl. Lord Tennyson noticed how she bit her lip.

Mr. Goody put his cap back on and looked down the road.

The children and Lord Tennyson went out onto the porch and followed his anxious look. The road was peaceful and clear of livestock.

"The water buffalo are mithing? Thith ith a terrible dithathter!" Tate said.

"They're not missing," Pearl said. "I just saw them."

They turned to look at her.

"When?" Mr. Goody asked.

"They just walked through our backyard. Baby Munch too. He was so cute. . . ."

"*What?*" Annie interrupted.

"Why didn't you say something?" Mary asked.

"I thought they were going for a walk," Pearl said,

shrinking under the stares of her brothers and sisters.

"Which direction did they go?" Mr. Goody asked. "You see, they're in danger just walking around. It could be a real disaster if they got on a busy road."

"Well, it was that way or . . . that way, I think," Pearl said, pointing one way and then the other.

"Pearl, think!" Ezra said.

But Pearl just burst into tears and buried her face in Lord Tennyson's fur.

"We can help look," Ezra said quickly.

"A thearch party!" Tate said. "Tho much more ekthiting than a movie!"

"No, no, but when do you expect your parents to be home?" Mr. Goody asked. "I can't ask children to go on a rescue mission."

A rescue mission! The children's faces lit up. They raced to their messy cubbies to pull their shoes on.

Lord Tennyson had a bad feeling in his stomach. He was proud of his children for wanting to help and giving up their movie night. But search parties often meant splitting up and not being able to watch all the children at once, especially with the parents away.

Mary grabbed her binoculars and spy notebook while Pearl and Tate found butterfly catchers and Ezra found a jump rope to use as a lasso.

"Kids?" they heard a voice say. Lord Tennyson turned at the sound—Mr. McNiff and Honey were home early, thank goodness!

Keeping Sweetums on his back, he trotted out to greet them.

The rest of the children followed, exploding with news about roaming buffalo.

"Never in my life did I think I would be participating in a water buffalo search party," Mr. McNiff said. He sniffed a dainty sniff and looked down at his spiffy shoes and striped linen pants.

"Who knowth what dangerth lurk in the foretht, right, Pearl?" Tate said.

Just then two tractors pulled into the driveway, carrying more neighbors, Shaw and Red. They hopped down.

"Heard Goody's buffalo are out," Shaw said.

"I told Goody they were nothin' but trouble," Red grumbled. "But does he listen to me?"

They eyed the sun, setting farther down into the horizon.

"You comin'?" Red asked Mr. McNiff.

"You betcha!" Mr. McNiff announced, marching dutifully behind the farmers. Lord Tennyson watched them walk into the woods, feeling torn between following with his superior nose or staying behind with the children.

"Pearl, what's the matter?" Honey asked. They sat down on the porch with Sweetums, and Honey pulled Pearl onto her lap.

"Baby Munch is lost," Pearl sniffed, clutching Nicholas. "And it's my fault, I couldn't remember which way she went! Munch is just a *baby!*"

"It's not your fault," Honey said reassuringly.

"The mama is missing," Pearl whispered to Nicholas. "What will the baby do without her?" Pearl slid off her mother's lap and grabbed Lord Tennyson around the neck. "We have to go find the mama!"

Lord Tennyson shook his head.

"Remember how I saved the bunnies?"

Lord Tennyson sniffed, nose to the ground, smelling only Widdy Boo and Nuff by the chicken coop.

"I *wanted* to save Lavinia, but . . ." Pearl was becoming emotional, and Lord Tennyson did not want to talk about

Lavinia. "And I wanted to save that boy, but that ladder was so high. I can find Ms. Monet, Tenny! I have to be brave! Remember how I saved the bunnies?"

He would reflect on and agonize over this moment, the last time he saw her. After he had dismissed her too easily. How had he missed how determined she was to be brave?

She walked to the edge of the backyard, looking out at the woods while Lord Tennyson ran back and forth in front of her, sniffing for a trail.

"We have to find them!" Pearl said each time he passed.

He became distracted as Mary and Annie, despite their relative peace these last few weeks, started to argue—which way they should go, how a jump rope might catch a buffalo, and whether Mary could ride one like a horse.

Finally, Tate, who was watching Sweetums on the porch while Honey went to call more neighbors, began jumping up and down. "He'th got one!"

It was true. Mr. Goody emerged from the woods leading a large buffalo. It was Rembrandt, with his silky, sleek black fur. Coming up behind them was Mr. McNiff, walking carefully so as not to get mud on his pants, a triumphant look on his face. He was holding on to a long rope that led into the woods. The closer he came, the more they could see whom he was leading—Baby Munch!

Mary snorted a laugh as Mr. McNiff tried to tip-toe around Rembrandt's large buffalo poop patty. Unfortunately, instead he slipped on the grass and landed on top of it.

The children fell over laughing.

"You got him, Dad!" Ezra said.

Mr. McNiff got up slowly and sniffed his shirt.

"Thanks, neighbor," Mr. Goody said, taking the rope from Mr. McNiff and patting him on the shoulder.

"Where'th Mith Monet?" Tate asked.

"She wouldn't leave her baby," Mary said.

"Must have gotten separated somehow," Mr. Goody said, sounding uneasy. "She's bound to be close."

At the mention of his mother, the calf let out a mournful moo.

A group gathered on the back porch as Mrs. Gage came walking around the house. And with her—the slinking Fat Cat. What did *she* want? Lord Tennyson growled at Fat Cat, still smarting from the scratch she had given him.

As usual, Fat Cat acted as if he were a speck of dirt,

swishing her fluffy white tail so close to him that her dander-filled hair caught in his nose. He exhaled forcefully, most ungentlemanlike.

Fat Cat purred but didn't leave. She hung around, suspiciously, as if she had information. Lord Tennyson snorted. He'd never known Fat Cat to be helpful.

She purred again, this time more insistently.

Lord Tennyson's ears perked up.

He looked carefully at Fat Cat.

Did she know something about Ms. Monet?

He barked for her to hurry up and tell him. Night was descending as quickly as the temperature. This was a dire situation, meaning *very bad*. He looked at Baby Munch. Munch mooed again for his mother, too young to be left on his own.

Lord Tennyson put his nose to the ground and began to sniff once again, but with all the people gathered, all the scents were beginning to meld into one.

Meanwhile, the farmers were holding a conference. Honey, Mr. McNiff, and Mrs. Gage were answering questions from the children but forbidding any of them to go into the woods in the dark.

"I'll wear my headlamp!" Ezra said.

"I'll thtay with Pearl and be thooper brave," Tate said fearfully. "Pearl?"

"Actually, it's past your bedtime," Honey said.

Lord Tennyson agreed.

"But, Mom!" Mary said. "We don't *all* have to go to bed with the babies."

Sweetums, being held by Honey, whacked Mary atop the head.

"Ow!"

"And we can't just forget about Ms. Monet!" Annie said.

"Mr. and Mrs. McNiff," Mr. Goody interrupted, "I'd be much obliged if someone could walk Rembrandt and Munch back home."

The children leaped up, eager to at least escort the mighty buffalo home.

"I'll do it," Mary said, swinging her handmade lasso.

"With your jump rope?" Annie asked. "Let *me* do it!"

"I'll lasso *you*!" Mary yelled.

"We'll ALL do it!" Ezra said, glaring at them both.

Mr. McNiff accompanied the older children and

the water buffalo down the street while shushing their argument.

"The old boy might be useful in the woods," Shaw commented.

It took Lord Tennyson a moment to realize *he* was being referred to as "the old boy."

"Tenny!" Sweetums howled from over her mother's shoulder.

"Go ahead," Honey said to him, carrying Sweetums and leading Tate into the house. "But you all be careful out there with Lord Tennyson. I hear the coyotes."

Lord Tennyson trembled.

Sweetums yelled, and Lord Tennyson silently promised he would be back as soon as possible to tuck her into bed. Tate, looking worried, followed his mother.

"Pearl?" he yelled in the house.

Prrrr.

Lord Tennyson turned to see Fat Cat again. Why was she bothering him? And what did she have in her mouth? A bird? Was she really coming to gloat now? He was struck with a great urge to chase the furball up a tree. Instead, he nodded formally to show her what social graces looked like.

Fat Cat took his stiff acknowledgment as an invitation to sidle up closer, smelling like such a *cat*.

Suddenly he saw what was in Fat Cat's mouth. It was Nicholas! She dropped him in front of Lord Tennyson.

He looked sharply at Fat Cat.

Pearl! Had Fat Cat *eaten* his Pearl?

Fat Cat meowed in protest until he finally understood what the furry feline was trying to tell him.

You have a child missing.

CHAPTER TWENTY

A Missing McNiff

HE WAS SUDDENLY FRANTIC, WILDLY ACCOUNTING FOR each McNiff, determined to prove that Fat Cat was wrong.

When was the last time he had seen Pearl?

Suddenly, Lord Tennyson heard a tremendous howl. He jumped a foot. The coyotes!

"Mmmmooooo," came the sound again. It wasn't a coyote at all, but Ms. Monet, muddy and wet, walking up the path on her own!

He was so relieved, he nearly wilted. The water buffalo were safe and found. Surely Pearl would be close behind, triumphant in her bravery.

Mr. Goody and Shaw were at the buffalo's side immediately. Ms. Monet shook out her fur, raining muddy water on all of them.

Lord Tennyson hardly noticed the dirty water, nor did he celebrate. Where was Pearl?

She did not emerge.

He circled the house.

"What's the matter, boy?" Ezra asked, coming back from up the street with Mary and Annie.

Lord Tennyson ran to a tired-looking Honey, who was just emerging from the house. She was holding Tate's hand. Tate had the same worried expression on his face.

"Where'th Pearl?" Tate asked. "Where'th my Pearl?"

Honey cocked her head to the side.

· "Tenny?"

"What's the matter?" Mr. McNiff asked.

He dropped Nicholas at their feet.

Mary and Annie gasped at the same time.

"Pearl," Honey whispered as her eyes rested on each of her children and came up one short.

Tate broke free from his mother and ran to the edge of the porch.

He opened his mouth and yelled—"MY PEARL, WHERE ARE YOU!"

At that moment they heard it. From deep in the forest came the familiar, loud, piercing sound of howling.

Pearl was missing.

And the coyotes were out.

Lord Tennyson wanted to comfort Honey, Mr. McNiff, and the other children, but there was no time. He began combing the large yard and the neighboring one, looking everywhere, not even tempted by the chickens. The other children looked too, calling Pearl's name in every inch of the backyard.

He had thought his greatest duty had been to help the McNiffs learn to be upstanding citizens and prove his worth as a nanny. But at that moment he would have been happy to be ignored, even out of a job, with all the children stomping in the mud and making trouble—as long as they were safe and together.

"I'm so sorry," Mr. Goody said, stricken, when Lord Tennyson came back without Pearl. "If Rembrandt and Ms. Monet hadn't escaped, none of this would have happened."

"I told her we can't do everything together," Tate said, his voice wobbling. "And now Pearl'th thumwhere without me!"

"Did you see her go?" Annie demanded.

"No!" Tate began to cry.

"I'm sorry, Tatey. I'm just scared. Come here."

Annie opened the blanket that she, Ezra, and Mary were huddling under on the steps of the back porch for Tate to come in. They were holding dimmed flashlights, their voices hoarse and hurting from calling their sister's name. An awful gloom hung heavily over them.

They heard a thump, a sliding down the stairs, and padding across the kitchen floor. Sweetums emerged, crawling over to Tenny and biting his tail.

"We have to call the police," Honey said.

"Sibling Council comes to order," Annie whispered. "We need to think very carefully. We know Pearl better than anyone. Where would she go?"

279

Annie, Ezra, Mary, Tate, and Sweetums squished together, and Lord Tennyson sat tensely in the middle of the circle.

"Maybe she climbed up a tree for the night," Mary said. "She's been trying to climb the crab apple tree in the backyard."

"Maybe she's upstairs sleeping," Ezra said.

"Mom already checked," said Annie.

"The forest? But it's so dark in there," Mary cried. "She would be too scared."

"We were fighting," Annie said guiltily. "So we lost track of her."

Ezra put his arm around her shoulders.

"She was my buddy," Mary said. "I was in charge of her and I only wanted to ride Rembrandt instead. It's my fault." Mary buried her head in her arms.

"It could have happened to any of us," Annie said, hugging her. "How often have I lost Sweetums?"

Mary hiccupped.

The police soon arrived, along with a slew of volunteers, but Lord Tennyson wouldn't wait for them. He knew the fault rested with him and him alone. He was Pearl's nanny and had taken his eyes off her. But he also knew Pearl's scent and habits better than anyone. He had lost her and would find her again.

He also knew he must explore every possibility and ask every creature what they knew and what they had seen, even the feline he liked least—Fat Cat.

Picking up Nicholas, he ran across the yard, looking for the cat. He circled the swing set, then stopped abruptly at the tree line, where Fat Cat had given him Nicholas. His Pearl was shy and afraid of the dark and would *never* go into the woods alone.

And yet. He remembered her insistent voice and all she had accomplished this summer.

She *had* ridden that bike.

She *had* reached the teapot.

She *had* volunteered to climb the ladder to save Curtis Cornell.

Wasn't it Pearl who loved animals most, who always wanted to rescue them?

And wasn't it he who had pushed her to have courage? To do hard things?

A cold fear came across Lord Tennyson.

He *had* to find her.

Fat Cat sauntered alongside him, stopping by the treehouse near a path leading into the forest. Was this where Pearl had gone?

It made sense; that's why she'd left Nicholas behind. For Lord Tennyson to find him—and her.

Fat Cat confirmed it with a swish of her tail.

He was actually hoping Fat Cat would search with him, but she was already slinking away from the forest, giving him a pitying look.

He would have to go alone—and fast.

Lord Tennyson put his nose to the ground, ready to set off.

But before leaving, he heard his name.

He paused.

"Lord Tennyson."

It was a mother's voice. Just like his mother's, when they had parted all those years ago.

"Lord Tennyson."

He turned, and there was Honey. Even in the dark he could see that her eyes and the tip of her nose were red.

She knelt in front of him, eye to eye. Putting her hands

around his face, she stroked his beard. "Lord Tennyson, we've relied on you so much—maybe too much, and I'm sorry. Can I ask one last thing of you? Can you find our Pearl?" It sounded like a prayer, the most important prayer that had ever come from her lips.

Lord Tennyson looked her in the eyes. Of course he would find her.

She hugged him tightly.

Mr. McNiff and the children, seeing Honey, joined her.

"Good boy, Tenny," Annie said.

"You're a born hunting dog!" Mary said.

"Of course he can do it," said Ezra.

Mr. McNiff held his paw. It was the firm handshake he needed. "The search party will be right behind you."

"Go, Tenny, go," Tate shouted. "Find my Pearl."

"Mine!" Sweetums yelled.

With that, he was off, alert and sniffing, to find his little Pearl.

CHAPTER TWENTY-ONE

Pearl

LORD TENNYSON SNIFFED AND SEARCHED FOR HOURS, seeking Pearl's scent on every leaf, blade of grass, and unturned rock. He hated to admit it, but he had lost Pearl's scent at the edge of the creek. Taking a drink from the creek bed, he shivered at the thought of crossing it. He detested swimming, though he knew he'd plunge across an ocean if he had to.

He gazed across the creek. Had Pearl seen Ms. Monet

or Baby Munch in the water? Why hadn't she followed them back? The search party must be in the woods now too. He heard their distant calls of her name. Why hadn't anyone seen her? Why had no one heard her cry? This was the most puzzling piece of all. Pearl was quiet, but she would cry if she was scared. Lord Tennyson had hoped to come across a squirrel or chipmunk for information, but alas, his presence had forced them to scurry into their little homes underground and inside tree trunks.

Another thought occurred to him, one he'd been trying to avoid, one that distressed and sent chills to his very core. She was not an especially strong swimmer. Had Pearl walked into the knee-length water? But why? And then what?

Lord Tennyson emerged from his thoughts to find himself face-to-face with a small vole. Voles, like mice, only slightly larger, were the bane of the McNiffs' front yard, as they loved to burrow underneath tree roots during the winter, emerging with spring to create long tunnels of dirt across the earth. Lord Tennyson found voles tasty. Not as much as birds, but a satisfying second.

The vole let out a high-pitched squeak as if it could

read Lord Tennyson's thoughts and quickly pushed a small dark object at him—one of Nicholas's shoes! Its eyes darted at the water—a clue. Pearl's scent disappeared at the water's edge for a reason. Out of thanks, Lord Tennyson did not pounce, and the vole scampered away.

He sniffed the shoe, sure that it was purposely dropped by his clever Pearl. She wanted him to find it. He gave three sharp barks. He didn't hear Pearl, but he did hear something. He peered across the creek again. Lord Tennyson was suddenly not alone. Where once there was only darkness on the other side of the water, now he saw what the children had always feared: wolves.

But as his eyes adjusted further, he realized they were not wolves at all, but a pack of coyotes.

They stood silently watching him. There were four of them, each with amber eyes. Three had matted gray fur, while one was a spotted brown with a cream-colored underbelly. The alpha male eyed him intensely, while his alpha mate bared her teeth.

Lord Tennyson would normally not engage with such mongrels as these. Although he had little experience with coyotes, he assumed they cared nothing for order or manners, only looking out for their own survival, certainly not the survival or raising of six human children. Plus, Pearl would be *terrified* by the sight of them. A panic rose within his chest. He asked the question again: Why hadn't he heard her crying?

But to find Pearl, he didn't have a choice. He had to cross the creek and talk to the coyotes.

He stuck one tip of his paw as gentlemanly as possible into the water. *Brrr.* It was August, yet the tree cover was so thick the sunlight rarely reached the water to warm it. Two of the coyotes backed up, but the female alpha gave a howl, either to warn Lord Tennyson or to call the rest of the pack. Lord Tennyson thought of Pearl and forced himself forward, launching himself into the cold water. He swam as gracefully across the creek as possible, trying not to get his goatee wet. He felt ridiculous, his legs furiously moving as his head bobbed above the water in what humans called a "doggy paddle."

The alphas made no sounds, just fixed their deep eyes on Lord Tennyson until he was all the way across.

As a show of good faith, Lord Tennyson bowed his head in greeting, then shook the water from his body.

His tongue hung out of his mouth as he gasped for air.

The coyotes were immediately upon him, sniffing every inch of him in the most intrusive manner! But he returned the action, sniffing for Pearl's scent. He was startled but sure: they had been with Pearl.

The male alpha blinked slowly before turning to his comrades. They exchanged a look before turning back to Lord Tennyson. But the female bared her fangs and hissed, walking around his shivering body.

Lord Tennyson's heart plummeted in his chest, and his bark to ask them to point him in the right direction died in his throat. Something was amiss.

Suddenly, she leaped toward him, an impressive, fluid jump that took him by surprise. With one quick motion she pinned him to the ground. It was even worse than Curtis Cornell.

Her mate barked, and she reluctantly let him up, but not before biting him sharply on his leg—*much* harder than Sweetums ever had.

Lord Tennyson yelped and looked down. His leg was bleeding. He was cold, tired, and very much afraid of this wild pack. In addition, he was far too old to fight.

Yet he rose from the ground, stiff and shivering, ready to do what he must.

Surprising him, the pack turned and walked away. He waited until they were a safe distance ahead, then followed them and the scent of Pearl on or close to them.

A half mile later, they were much farther into the forest than Lord Tennyson had ever been, which admittedly was not saying much. They came upon a cave of semi-fallen trees, where younger coyote pups romped and wrestled. This must be their den. But he saw something lying on the ground—Nicholas's other shoe. And it had more teeth marks on it.

Frantic but silent, Lord Tennyson followed the pack until he heard the sweetest voice he could have ever heard—"Tenny! Oh, Tenny!"

All at once Pearl was on him, smiling and hugging him so tightly around his neck, he thought he might suffocate. He didn't mind; he would never mind again.

He licked Pearl on both cheeks. She was dirty but safe, with no apparent injuries. How, he wondered, had she survived the night so far? His eyes caught the entrance to the den. The coyotes. She must have slept with them for warmth. How easily she had become their pup. Her gentleness and love had surely kept her safe. For the first time in his life, he felt an odd glimmer of appreciation for these uncouth dogs.

The female alpha growled, broke free of the pack, and stood protectively by Pearl.

Pearl timidly reached her hand out to touch the female's nose, and the coyote softened.

My goodness, this was almost straight out of that *Jungle Book* story.

Lord Tennyson looked at the sky, at the sun that was beginning to rise.

"I don't want to go home, Tenny." Pearl yawned. "I have to find the water buffalo. Take me to find them, Tenny."

They began to walk back the way Lord Tennyson had come, and most of the coyotes showed no interest in whether they stayed or not. Except for one. The alpha female. She growled, baring sharp teeth and separating the two of them.

The other coyotes circled their sleeping area before lying down, watching the standoff between Lord Tennyson and the alpha as she wound her body around Pearl's.

They weren't leaving anytime soon.

So Lord Tennyson and Pearl lay down in the den, the alpha female in between them, and Lord Tennyson tried to think of a plan. But his tired mind could think of nothing but his achy, exhausted joints and the pain in his leg. He did not want to sleep, not here among the coyotes, but he had found Pearl and would need strength to get her home. So finally, he allowed himself to drift into a light slumber. He had often thought the McNiff children were wild animals, but for the first time in his life, Lord Tennyson truly slept among the wild dogs.

Not long after, he awoke with a start—Pearl was lost!

But no, she was now curled up beside the alpha like a coyote pup. He could feel her breath as she stirred. Lord Tennyson's leg was aching and sore from the bite, probably getting infected from the mongrel's lack of dental care. His fur was tangled with blood, briars, and mud. He frowned at his appearance; what a mess he would be for Mr. McNiff to comb out. His stomach growled, and Pearl's stomach echoed it. He must get her home to Honey and her family.

Lord Tennyson eyed the female alpha, who appeared to be sleeping with one eye open between him and Pearl. But when he moved, she didn't stir.

Could he get Pearl home without a fight? He crawled on his belly a few paces.

The sun was up. And outside the den, standing on a large rock, was a sight that made him catch his breath. The leader of the pack stood majestically, the sun bathing his fur so that it shone almost blue. Sensing Lord Tennyson, he turned slightly but not to stop him. Lord Tennyson realized he was telling him to go.

He crawled back around to Pearl, softly nudging her. When she didn't wake, he became more insistent, pulling on her shirt with his teeth until finally she opened her eyes.

She yawned, and her stomach growled again. He put a paw to Pearl's mouth to keep her quiet. She nodded. The alpha female did not wake.

Holding tightly to his collar, she tiptoed beside him through the large overgrowth, back toward home. Every step away from the coyote den was a step closer to safety.

As they traveled, Pearl frequently tripped on sticks and was scratched on her face and arms. Lord Tennyson comforted her by rubbing his nose on her legs and licking her cheeks, and she traveled quietly, without complaint. He checked behind him often to make sure they weren't being followed, then concentrated on sniffing his way back to the creek.

Lord Tennyson was exultant when they finally found their way to the water. If he could get them both across, he was certain he could pick up a scent and get them home from there. Pearl whimpered when she stepped into the cold water and it splashed up against her thighs. He nudged her forward. He jumped in after her, and the cold water stung badly on his injured leg. So badly that it was Pearl who assisted Lord Tennyson across the creek as he paddled with his head just barely above the water, not the other way around.

As the water lapped at his nose and stung his eyes, he heard the first sounds of the female alpha noticing their absence. A howl of fury, then another, growing nearer. The other coyotes joined in like a rich and layered symphony, but it was the female who rose above the others. Was it his imagination, or was her song tinged with the great longing for a child?

Lord Tennyson swam harder.

Pearl was *his* child. Whether the McNiffs got a new nanny or not. She would always be his.

He paddled until Pearl put her arm around Lord Tennyson and helped him up onto shore on the other side of the creek. They pressed forward, until they could no longer hear the howls drawing closer, until the brush became lighter, and until finally, the big pink farmhouse on Marigold Lane was in sight.

CHAPTER TWENTY-TWO

Truly McNifficent

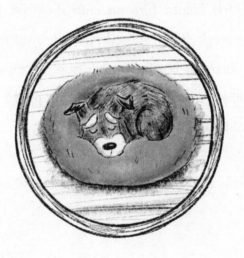

IT WAS EARLY MORNING WHEN THEY EMERGED AND saw the rest of the children. He could hear others in the forest and was gratified that there were people still searching for them. But there was no greater gratification than seeing the McNiffs.

"Ten Ten!" Sweetums shrieked. "Ten!"

"Ith that my Pearl?" Tate asked.

Lord Tennyson saw Honey and Mr. McNiff look up,

eyes bloodshot with worry, hair and clothes a mess from searching the forest and being up all night. Honey gasped.

"Oh, thank goodness!" Mr. McNiff said.

A crowd of volunteers looking at a map turned.

"Is that a *dog* or a *rat*?" Lord Tennyson heard someone say. He was too tired to protest.

They all ran toward them.

Lord Tennyson limped forward. Still holding on to his collar was his precious, bedraggled Pearl. In her other hand she clutched Nicholas's shoe. Soon the entire town seemed to be grabbing her and passing her around until she was in the arms of her mother and father.

"Oh, my sweet Pearl," Honey said.

After hugging and kissing their sister, the children came for Lord Tennyson. He never thought he would be so glad to be suffocated by crying children.

"Oh, Tenny," Mary cried.

Ezra pulled him onto his lap even though his fur was soaked through and knotted with mud, stickers, and slime from the creek. He lay in Ezra's lap, drifting toward a place of sleep and rest.

"Tenny boy," Mr. McNiff said, stroking his fur. "There

never was a better boy than you." He didn't say "old boy," but that's how Lord Tennyson felt.

"Let me hold him," Annie cried, but Ezra wouldn't let him go.

"What'th the matter with Tenny?" Tate said. "Why ithn't he moving?"

"He's worn out," Mr. McNiff said. "He'll feel and look better after a nap and a shower."

Normally Lord Tennyson would run away at the mention of a shower, but he barely heard the words.

The McNiff parents took Pearl to the hospital, where she was checked out and deemed "remarkably resilient" upon release, while Dr. Weber, the town veterinarian, came to see Lord Tennyson. But he did not want attention now. He did not want to eat or drink, even though he was both hungry and very thirsty, cold, and shaking. All he wanted was to nap in the sun for a very long time, smelling the sweet smell of lilac bushes.

Dr. Weber took his heart rate, stroked his hair, and looked at the children. He had a very serious expression on his face.

He paused. "You'll need to keep a close eye on the wound

on his leg and give him his medicine," he said, touching his bandaged leg. "Lord Tennyson also needs to stay warm and get a lot of rest. He needs to keep drinking water, and . . . well, this is a serious situation for a senior dog."

"What do you mean?" Mary asked.

"Ith Tenny going to . . . Puppy Planet?" Tate asked. Before anyone could answer the question, he burst into tears.

Pearl threw herself on top of Lord Tennyson as the rest huddled around. He wanted to reassure them, but he couldn't even muster a bark.

"I'm not saying that," the vet said hastily. "Let him rest, and take good care of him."

Lord Tennyson drifted into sleep then, thinking of a summer that was now almost past. He wondered if he had accomplished what he had set out to do a mere few months ago. Were the McNiffs any more well mannered and prepared for the challenges of the world around them? He could recall every disaster much more acutely than any win, especially the last one. Thank goodness Pearl was safe. At least he could feel good about loving them enough to try.

And then, throughout the day, he witnessed quite a

remarkable thing. The children stepped up in a way Lord Tennyson had only dreamed of. They brought him water, tried to feed him, coaxed him to move. They gave him medicine and warned one another to be gentle when touching. He was never left alone. It was a role reversal he had never considered—them taking care of him.

Even though they had an ABC belching contest to "cheer Tenny up," they were thinking of others (of him) more than themselves. During the day Pearl read him books, while Tate told jokes. Ezra wrestled both a tutu and the toenail clippers away from Sweetums when she approached (a show of love from both of them, in their own way). Annie never once called Mary a "rat," and Mary only spoke in soft tones. All this, he observed, was for him.

That evening the children were sent to bed early. But without Lord Tennyson tucking them in, no one could sleep. Pearl tossed around in bed until finally she crept downstairs. Ezra and Mary were already there. Soon after, Tate and Annie came, followed by Sweetums sliding down the stairs by her diaper. Together they slept huddled like the coyotes in the woods, next to Lord Tennyson in the living room.

"You are a true brother," Ezra whispered. "The best brother a boy could ever have. And once you get better, you will move into my room with Tate."

"Oh, goody goody gumdropth," Tate said.

"Without me?" Pearl asked.

"Don't worry," Tate said. "I'll thtill be around."

Lord Tennyson weakly blinked twice. He felt a small rise of happiness, but also a fading, a tiredness beyond sleep.

Lord Tennyson was drifting. Where, he wondered, was he going?

And then he felt he understood. He was an old dog who had lived a good life. There was no other family he would have wanted to live it with. And in his heart he knew he had done his very best, even if all his grand plans had more than occasionally backfired. They were not perfect children, but he was glad for that, too. Weren't their antics and personalities part of their charm?

At that moment Pearl whispered, "All dogs go to heaven, Tenny. But especially you."

He heard sniffles. Lord Tennyson did not want them to be sad. They had had a wonderful life together. The children were resisting as they always did, but this time Lord Tennyson did not feel like scolding them.

He vaguely heard the three eldest talking to him, but he couldn't make out the words. Ezra, Annie, and Mary. It was time for them to step up and teach the little ones all he had taught them. He realized that what he was feeling was what humans called love. His one regret was that perhaps they did not know how much of it he had for them.

"You were always the truest, kindest, and best dog anyone could ever hope for," Annie said, stroking his fur. "Even though you ate Lavinia."

"Tenny, I love you," Tate said, grabbing his neck a little too roughly.

Mary slung her arm over his middle.

"I'm sorry I was so naughty all the time. I'll be a better girl, Tenny, I promise. No more trouble. No more fights. Just please get better. Oh, please, Tenny boy."

"Come on, children," he heard Honey say. "Let him rest."

The children protested, but then Honey was kneeling beside his bed. She rearranged his favorite blanket and stroked his beard just the way he liked.

"Dear Tenny," she whispered. "Thank you. We've needed you so much."

He blinked long and hard at his beloved Honey. He almost chuckled at hearing the words he'd longed for all summer. All this time, he had only thought it was *they* who needed *him*. Why, he needed them, too. After all, that's how it worked in a family. Perhaps he was not just a nanny after all, but an actual McNiff. The thought was wonderful, but it also made him sadder to be leaving.

Lord Tennyson was tired.

He closed his eyes.

"Dad," Ezra whispered. "Can't we do anything?"

"It's up to Tenny now," Mr. McNiff said.

Honey herded the children away. The rabbits, Delilah and Felicity, hopped over, paying their respects by giving him a good sniffing.

Lord Tennyson couldn't resist the deep sleep anymore. Just before he let go, though, Mr. McNiff, his great mister, leaned over and gave Lord Tennyson the gift he had always wanted. "Thank you, my friend," he whispered. "Thank you for your years of service. You were, and always will be, truly McNifficent."

CHAPTER TWENTY-THREE

What Heaven Feels Like

LORD TENNYSON OPENED HIS EYES.

He could hear the chirping birds he liked so much, but he felt too weary to chase them. Maybe this afternoon. He blinked twice from the bright light shining in his eyes. He stretched, yawned, and decided he was hungry.

He looked around his surroundings, but the light was so bright he could not make out where he was.

Then yesterday began flooding back to him and he realized.

Heaven. It was so peaceful he must be in heaven. Or maybe it was Tate's Puppy Planet—but then where were all the puppies? Perhaps it was good there were none. It was quiet. So quiet he could nap all day! He could go under a porch somewhere. Surely they had porches in heaven?

Was his name still Lord Tennyson? He hoped so. He rather liked his name. Was his mother here? His brothers and sisters? The thought cheered him, but only for a second.

It was quiet and peaceful, just like he had always longed for, but . . . too quiet. Would a nap hold the same satisfaction without a rambunctious family of squirrelly children to wake him? Would he even want to ride a bike with no one to pedal with? He wondered, did people go to the same place as their dogs? Because he still wanted to inquire after a library card. And if they were coming, he wanted to wait for them.

Hearing a noise in the distance, he rose and stiffly limped across the floor, suddenly remembering he'd been bitten. That was strange. Wasn't he supposed to be healed in heaven? Lord Tennyson entered the next room, where he encountered a child. So there *were* humans here! She was sitting on the floor. She looked remarkably like Sweetums, with an angelic sprout of hair on top of her head. She was even doing what Sweetums loved to do early in the morning before Honey was up: lick brown sugar out of the Tupperware container.

He frowned, about to stop her out of habit, but second-guessed his response. She was not his child. Whose job was it to ensure that this child didn't get cavities? Unless . . . there were no cavities in heaven.

Out of principle, Lord Tennyson picked up the lid with his teeth and put it firmly back on the container with his paw. The little girl giggled and tugged on his hair just the way Sweetums used to do while he finagled the brown sugar out of her reach. He turned and licked the brown sugar off her fingers and cheeks. It tasted even more delicious than usual.

"Ten!" she said, hugging him around the middle. He almost fainted from the smell; this child needed a diaper change!

Lord Tennyson stepped back and observed the child.

He slowly and carefully licked her cheek again. She tasted like Sweetums. She had the same blueberry eyes and curls as Sweetums. How odd. Could it be possible . . . ?

His thoughts were interrupted by a great thundering sound, just like the unholy thundering of children on the stairs in the McNiffs' pink house at 238 Marigold Lane. Then two children who looked remarkably like Pearl and Tate rushed at him, followed by Annie, Mary, and Ezra look-alikes. They made loud whooping, unmannerly noises just like the McNiffs.

"Mama!" the small boy with red rubber glasses yelled. "Tenny'th not dead!"

Not dead? Had he really survived? He wasn't in Puppy Planet? These children . . . were really his children? They petted and pulled at him. They stepped on his toenails, and the baby grabbed his ears. They had no respect for space and boundaries.

But it was when Mary and Annie began to argue over breakfast that he was sure: Lord Tennyson was very much alive in the McNiffs' disorganized kitchen with that ever-growing Osbert character still on the counter.

And then Honey and Mr. McNiff appeared.

While Honey and Mr. McNiff rushed to him, something happened that Lord Tennyson had never seen before. Annie hugged Mary and Mary hugged Ezra and Ezra hugged Pearl and Pearl hugged Tate *and* her Nicholas. It was a domino effect of love.

Perhaps his job was finished after all.

Then Sweetums crawled over and whacked them all with a spoon.

"Ow!" Annie yelled. "Tenny, make her stop!"

Mary belched loudly. "Sorry, Tenny."

"I can do it better," Ezra said. And he did.

Well, perhaps not.

"I'll be in the garden," Honey sang.

Ah, yes. Honey needed him this morning, and likely tomorrow, too. She and Mr. McNiff would probably forget to feed the children breakfast tomorrow if he didn't remind them. Annie was getting boy crazy and needed a reminder to be patient and kind. Mary was repentant at the moment, but what about tomorrow? Ezra needed to speak up at Sibling Councils, to start deodorizing his sneakers—and to stop trying to keep pet snakes. Pearl, who had now survived a coyote's den, needed to take her newfound confidence into starting kindergarten this fall on her own. Tate was about to sprout out of Ezra and Pearl's shadow, but he needed practice saying his *s*'s. As for baby Sweetums? She would never survive the beach without him.

His children *had* made progress that summer—he'd seen it, if only in glimpses, but there was still much to do.

Lord Tennyson hauled Sweetums out to the porch and set her down. He lay with his head on her lap. *Oh dear, a diaper change, please!* But Sweetums quieted down and sucked on his ear.

"Kids," he heard Mr. McNiff say through the kitchen window. "The kitchen is a mess . . . but it's a very happy day."

Lord Tennyson couldn't help but agree. A happy day indeed.

As he sat in the sun, a list of to-dos was beginning to clutter his mind. The children still weren't properly flossing their back molars. How, he wondered, could such a thing be taught by a miniature schnauzer? He would, of course, figure it out as he always did. He was, after all, a rather spectacular dog.

But on this late-summer day at 7:12 in the morning,

Lord Tennyson put aside the flossing lesson. This morning he could only feel content. He was alive and back in the home of his family with an important and special role to play. Just like everyone who has ever been born into a family.

No, his task was not an easy one, as worthwhile work never is, but they'd never fire him, or send him away. He was loved and he was wanted. And together, they were a McNifficent family indeed. That felt good enough for a thousand days.

Acknowledgments

The author would like to acknowledge:

The readers: thank you for reading this book! I hope it made you laugh and also love and appreciate the family (and furry friends) around you.

The teachers, librarians, and booksellers who work so hard to get books into the hands of readers—you are gold!

Andrea and Kim, my sisters and first readers, for the many reading rounds in the early years. And also my nieces and nephews for listening at bedtime, laughing at the right parts, and insisting that the chicken legs stay.

Julia Tomiak, aka the Word Nerd, for reading early drafts, always checking in, and cheerleading.

The Brain Trust. Here's to strong, thinking, creative women.

My wonderful neighbors and neighborhood, which inspired many of the characters and animals, as well as the setting, in this story. A special shout-out to Jim Goody!

John Bytheway and his superb storytelling. Your "riding the family bike" analogy made such an impression that the McNiffs are now (working on) riding their family bike together too.

Phenomenal literary agent Zoe Sandler, who works tirelessly on my behalf; I am so grateful, and I hope Baby A will someday read and love this book.

My editor, Alexa Pastor, who dives into every draft with such thoroughness and care, making every book better. Thank you!

Ariel Landy, for capturing the McNiffs with such on-point illustrations, and the entire team at Simon & Schuster Children's for their extraordinary efforts.

My mother, Mary, who inspired our dear Naughty Mary in so many ways. And my dad, Steven Nelson, who acts as my official and unofficial publicist by handing out my books as soon as you ring the doorbell.

My beloveds: Cope, Nelson, Brynne, and Paige, who give me such terrific real-life material to work with, and Gregor, best supporting partner ever. I love you.

And of course, Lord Tennyson, who not only inspired the great dignified nanny in this story, but who has truly been the best playmate and child-tamer we've ever had—pink tutus and all.